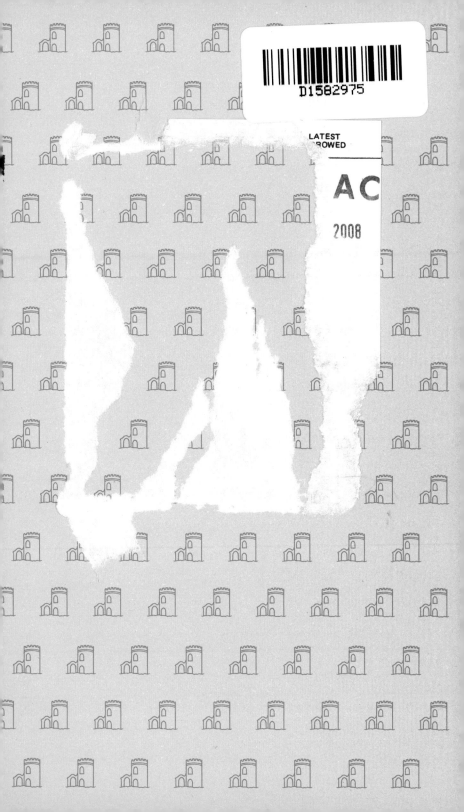

D1582975

Love is
a time of enchantment:
in it all days are fair and all fields
green. Youth is blest by it,
old age made benign:
the eyes of love see
roses blooming in December,
and sunshine through rain. Verily
is the time of true-love
a time of enchantment — and
Oh! how eager is woman
to be bewitched!

MASTER OF MALCAREW

When Helen receives a plea for help from her old college friend, Margaret, she travels at once to Malcarew. Grudgingly received at the brooding old house by the brothers Roland and Patrick, Helen is drawn into a complicated web of evil, involving not only Roland's wife and Patrick's fiancée, but other inhabitants of the rural community, who seek to re-enact an ancient wickedness. But it is on the downs above Malcarew that Helen, at last, learns the true nature of the master of Malcarew.

VERONICA BLACK

MASTER OF MALCAREW

Complete and Unabridged

ULVERSCROFT
Leicester

First published in Great Britain in 1971 by
Robert Hale Limited
London

First Large Print Edition
published February 1995
by arrangement with
Robert Hale Limited
London

British Library CIP Data

Black, Veronica
  Master of Malcarew.—Large print ed.—
Ulverscroft large print series: romance
I. Title
823.914 [F]

ISBN 0–7089–3233–9

4/98

073790051

Published by
F. A. Thorpe (Publishing) Ltd.
Anstey, Leicestershire
Set by Words & Graphics Ltd.
Anstey, Leicestershire
Printed and bound in Great Britain by
T. J. Press (Padstow) Ltd., Padstow, Cornwall

This book is printed on acid-free paper

1

AT first, Margaret wrote fairly regularly and Helen was pleased when the neat, white envelopes plopped on to the mat. Despite the promises made, the addresses exchanged, few friendships had endured from training college days. It had been a closed and crowded world, a world of timetables, lectures, sessions in union, teaching practice, homespun philosophy over the coffee cups. At the time, it had seemed as if relationships forged then would last for ever, but inevitably the bonds had slackened. Most of the crowd in which Helen and Margaret moved had married; a few had gone abroad; one or two had drifted away from teaching into other careers. When they met at reunion dinners, they had become individuals grown beyond college chants and rag week stunts.

Margaret did not attend reunions. She had never made any secret of the fact that it was her intention to give up teaching the moment she found a man weak-minded enough to marry her.

"And you may keep your handsome paupers!" she had exclaimed in that blunt, no-nonsense manner people found less than attractive. "My husband will be very rich and very old. *Very* old!" she had repeated, rubbing her fingers as if she were brushing grave dust from them. Then she had laughed at Helen's faintly shocked expression.

"I wish you wouldn't say things like that," Helen had protested.

"Why not? Why shouldn't I be honest?" Margaret enquired. "I'm a plain-faced, healthy, fairly intelligent young woman. I may not be a thirty-year-old's dream of heaven, but I can cultivate a very effective bedside manner with elderly gentlemen. Mark me, but I'll be a rich widow while you're still wandering about with your idealistic head in the clouds and about sixpence in the bank!"

It was true, Helen supposed, and was aware that part of their friendship was based upon this difference in their characters. Margaret at twenty-two had

2

already cast a long, analytical look at her own potentialities. Helen at the same age was still trying to mould herself into a world that even then went too fast for her.

"You were born to lie languidly on a sofa and read yellow-backed novels," Michael teased her. "The Honourable Helen Clifford at Home."

"Instead of which I sit on a hard chair marking grubby exercise books!"

"Marry me, and we can mark them together." Michael swept the books aside and put his arms round her.

"Not yet, Michael. Not just yet." She allowed herself to be kissed and then moved away, straightening the exercise books.

"When then? When will you stop playing teacher and settle down to being a — "

"Wife and mother? Michael, I can't throw up my training in two minutes. My parents put me through college."

"Rubbish! You were awarded a handsome grant."

"Well, they allowed me to stay on at school long enough to qualify for a grant.

I must teach for a year or two. And you can't afford to get married yourself yet. Anyway I'm not sure," she said in a burst of irritation, "if I want to marry anybody. Don't hurry me. I hate to be rushed."

That had been a year before, when she had known Michael for six months. At that time Margaret's letters were still arriving every two or three months although it was three years since they had left college and two years since Margaret, between jobs, had breezed in for a weekend.

At that time she had announced her intention of doing some private coaching.

"Six weeks here, six months there. Who knows but I might meet some lonely widower grateful for the attention I lavish on his child's education?"

She had spoken jokingly, but there was the steady glint in her eyes that Helen remembered and half-envied. It was so different from her own gentle, almost timid glance.

"I'm never sure," Michael grumbled, "exactly what you're staring at but I'd like to see it one day."

"I'm looking at you," Helen said,

uncharacteristically flirtatious, but the answer was an evasion, although she could not have said what her glance might ever penetrate. It had been the same at school when her teachers accused her of day-dreaming, and she had turned her quiet blue eyes back to her book, knowing that without interruption she might have seen that faint, intangible world that lay beyond the realities of desk and window.

Margaret had found her rich and elderly widower, and announced their marriage in another of her square, neatly-written envelopes, on a single sheet of notepaper.

'As you may see from the heading and my new surname, dear Helen, I am now a married woman. My husband is a Mr. Donald Carew and our wedding took place very quietly a month ago. I did not inform anybody as Mr. Carew is in a very delicate state of health. Indeed, he is not expected to live very long. You will, I know, wish us some happiness.'

The letter had been headed simply,

> 'Malcarew,
> 'Linton,
> 'Wiltshire.'

Helen had sent a telegram of congratulations, and been still debating whether or not to follow it up with a gift, when a black-bordered funeral card had arrived, informing her that Mr. Donald Carew, born in eighteen-ninety-five, had passed away quietly in a London nursing home. At the bottom of the card, Margaret had penned neatly,

> 'Donald and I came to London two weeks ago to consult a specialist but he was taken ill again upon our arrival.'

"Seventy-five!" Helen had exclaimed to Michael. "Margaret's husband was fifty years older than she was."

"And presumably rich," Michael pointed out. "You can't get into that particular nursing home on the National Health. Your friend sounds as if she has her wits about her."

Michael had never met Margaret and was in the habit of talking about her as if she were some legendary creature.

"She was always — sensible," Helen agreed, and wondered why the thought should chill her a little. Margaret's good sense had always seemed an entirely admirable thing. She would, for example, never waste five minutes of her time on a grey-eyed, broad-shouldered architect called Michael Barron.

After that there had been a Christmas card, and then a highly-coloured postcard, of the Alps where Margaret was apparently on a ski-ing holiday, and then a short, briskly cheerful letter from Linton in Wiltshire, informing Helen that she was well and settling down comfortably. After that, there had been a fairly long silence. Helen had written twice and then, deciding that Margaret was severing the last threads of their friendship, not written again. And the silence had lasted until the square white envelope had again plopped on to the mat.

Helen picked it up with some eagerness but delayed opening it until she was drinking her coffee and eating the one

7

slice of toast she allowed herself. It was indirectly because of that meagre breakfast that she sat alone at the beginning of a weekend with nothing to do except open Margaret's letter.

The previous evening she and Michael had had one of their silliest, most trivial, most pointless and most hurtful quarrels. It had begun with Helen scowling at the spaghetti heaped on her plate by the waiter in the little trattoria they frequented. It had ended with Michael declaring furiously, that she could diet herself to death for all he cared while she struggled unaided into her coat, lowering her head so that the other customers wouldn't see her stubborn tears. She could not even recall exactly what arguments and recriminations had passed in choked, whispering voices across the checked tablecloth. Michael had been, she thought, infuriatingly bossy, intimating that he had a right even to dictate the food she ate. And she herself, Helen admitted now, had wilfully refused to see that his concern sprang from love, his interference from his need to become an integral part of her life.

They had parted without making any arrangements when next to meet, and though she was almost certain he would ring up, she was aware that their relationship would have to move on into marriage or else wither away. She was, she told herself sternly, a fool not to accept him at once. Nine out of ten women would agree with her. The tenth would be Margaret who would urge that Helen, with her looks, could do better.

Thinking of Margaret, Helen broke the seal on the letter and drew out the sheet of paper. Like all Margaret's letters, this one was short but scrawled so hastily that for an instant Helen scarcely recognized the handwriting. A glance at the envelope showed the same hasty letters. She had not noticed it when she first picked it up.

'Malcarew,
'Linton.
'17th April.

'Dear Helen,
'Would you come down and see me for a few days, now? I badly

9

need somebody. In this place only Phoebe is my friend. Don't write to confirm your visit. There is something here — '

The note broke off abruptly there as if the writer had been interrupted, but her initials were signed in the same hurried manner.

Helen drank her coffee without tasting it while she read the note a second and a third time. What in the world had possessed the self-contained and efficient Margaret to send such an appeal? She must have been very badly frightened not to remember that the summer term had just begun and Helen was simply not free to slip away for a few days. But frightened of what? Something more than loneliness had prompted this desperate appeal for company.

Helen went over to the telephone and dialled Directory Enquiries, but her question was fruitless. 'Malcarew' in Linton was not, the polite, impersonal voice assured her, on the telephone.

Helen replaced the receiver with a feeling of frustration, and then, lifting it again, dialled Michael's number. His landlady answered in a bright, friendly manner which makes almost any statement sound like a lie. Mr. Barron had gone to work early that morning and hadn't said anything about coming back for lunch. When Helen rang the office, the bell shrilled over and over into a blank silence.

She slammed down the receiver and swore under her breath at men who went off sulking because they couldn't get their own way, and at women who were foolish enough to phone round after them. Then she made fresh coffee and read the letter again.

Over the weekend indeed she read it several times, but it remained mysterious and frightening. Frightening, she decided, because it was so completely out of character. She tried Michael's office again twice without success, and then, more annoyed with herself than ever, pulled on her coat and went off to the local cinema where she spent a miserable afternoon watching a man who resembled Michael making love to a black-haired Italian beauty.

When she arrived home, there was a note lying on the mat.

'Called away up north until next weekend. Rush job, but big commission. Love you,'

ran Michael's slanting script.

It blurred as tears rushed into her eyes. Until that moment she had not realized how much she had counted upon Michael's reading Margaret's letter, and then putting the whole thing into perspective in a way that would make nonsense of her fears.

Fear was perhaps too strong a word for the formless anxieties that lay at the back of her mind and sometimes forced themselves into her conscious thoughts.

The next day dragged interminably though she deliberately kept herself occupied in cleaning the flat, clearing a backlog of marking, and washing and setting her hair. She hoped Michael would phone but evidently he was too busy. The conclusion she reached made her unreasonably angry, though she was well aware that he was occasionally sent off at short notice, usually to consult with somebody too busy to spare any day but Sunday for a junior architect.

That night she slept badly, which was unusual, as Helen was one of those fortunate people who sink into slumber within ten minutes and remain peacefully unaware until the shrilling of the alarm clock. This morning she slept through the alarm and had no time even for coffee. When she arrived at school, Assembly was already over and her own pupils were, to judge from the shrieks, engaged in a full-scale massacre.

She went in swiftly, ordering them back to their places, hearing her own voice harsh and high, seeing the children's faces fall and settle into stubborn resentment. Normally she enjoyed her work, but on this particular day her pupils had never seemed more stupid, more wilfully determined to create as much noise as possible. She was not, thank God, on playground duty, but by the time she had mopped up spilt ink and adjudged the rightful owner of a disputed ruler, the meagre twenty minutes was almost over and the coffee waiting in the staffroom was tepid.

"You don't look well this morning," Miss Webster said, in her kind, fussy manner.

Helen wanted to snap that a quarrel with her boy-friend, a nagging worry about an old friend, and a prolonged bout of slimming was hardly the formula for radiant health, but before she had uttered half a sentence, she found herself crying miserably, with the cup of cold coffee shaking in her hand and the other members of the staff hanging over her in alarm.

"Nerves," Miss Herbert said briskly, hiding concern as she gazed at one of her most valued members of staff. "You've been off colour for some time, my dear. Now, you'll go straight to your doctor during the lunch-hour and get him to order you a leave of absence. At least a week, I'd say. And don't bleat to me about the teaching shortage. We can replace you for a week with a supply teacher. And you can take a rest, somewhere quiet where there are no registers, no bells, no screaming infants.

We'll see you again in a fortnight, say."

The staff, rather less sympathetic now that they were faced with the prospect of adding her pupils to their own until the replacement arrived, watched her collect her things and depart guiltily, still dabbing her eyes.

The doctor, grumbling that she should have made an appointment, ran a cursory eye over her shadowed eyes and pallor, wrote out a prescription for an iron tonic, and informed her brusquely that young women who were meant to be Junos ought not to try to starve themselves into Echoes. Then, pleased by his own knowledge of antiquity, he tapped her on the shoulder and dismissed her rather more cordially.

And that, she thought, hurrying to the bank before it closed, was that. The following day she would catch the first available train and be at this place called Linton by lunchtime. Margaret would no doubt explain the meaning of her cryptic note, and it would all prove to be a simple matter. And that, Helen chided herself, is simply not true. Margaret would never have written so strangely had something not happened to jolt her quite out of her normal pattern of behaviour.

Because there was nothing better to do than sit tamely waiting for Michael to ring, she went out again in the evening, finding a masochistic pleasure in drinking innumerable cups of coffee at the trattoria where the waiter hovered paternally, evidently expecting Michael to rush in and stage a dramatic reconciliation.

On the way home, she made a detour to Michael's lodgings and gazed at the front door for several minutes while she debated whether or not to leave a note. Then she remembered that he would be away until the end of the week and by that time she would have returned herself. Two or three days would straighten out the problem of Margaret, and Helen could then sort out her own life which seemed, at the moment, to be pulling her in two directions at once.

She slept deeply as if to make up for the previous night, half-waking only once when her sleep-dogged brain tried to indicate that the telephone was ringing, but the impulse threaded along her

16

nerves and died before it reached her drowsy fingertips. Her half-raised hand fell back to the pillow, and memory was submerged in oblivion.

She awoke feeling so refreshed that her tears of the previous day seemed to belong to another age. It was not like her to give way to her emotions, and she could only assume that she was either more involved with Michael than she cared to admit, or more upset by her friend's trouble than she realized.

Although she had decided upon an early train, there was time for a bath before she drank her coffee. She dressed carefully, wondering if in the three years since they had met Margaret had forsaken her bright, cheaply stylish clothes for something more befitting a wealthy wife — widow, Helen corrected herself — and hoped Margaret would not pretend a grief she could not possibly be feeling.

When she was ready, with her suitcase packed and her camel coat over the matching dress, she decided she looked exactly like a schoolteacher going to spend a few days with a friend. Even the French pleat into which she habitually twisted her heavy yellow hair was spinsterish. She made a face at herself, picked up her suitcase and locked the door behind her.

The train was three-quarters empty and she was able to choose a corner-seat before it pulled away from the platform. Helen had provided herself with a magazine to while away the two hour journey but it rested unopened in her lap while, chin in hand, she watched the landscape slide past, and let the puzzling sentences of that hastily written note echo over and over in her mind, as regularly and meaninglessly as the wheels of the train.

They had informed her at the booking office that the branch-line at Linton was closed down, but that there was an excellent bus-service from Stansbury, and the ride itself no more than twenty minutes or so. When she alighted at the station, the squat green vehicle was already waiting beyond the barrier. About a dozen passengers were in their seats and a dozen pairs of eyes swivelled towards her as she lifted her suitcase to the top step.

The bus dipped down past thick green hedges and then spiralled up towards rows of raw brick houses set down like toys in the surrounding turf. The conductor lounged down the aisle towards her with no gleam of interest in his face at the sight of a stranger. When she asked him to put her down at Linton, he nodded slowly without changing his expression, but she heard whispers at her back.

The journey took half-an-hour, and Helen was apparently the only one bound for Linton, as passengers got off the bus at every stop and their places were not filled. By the time they rattled into a small cobbled square, she and the taciturn incurious conductor were alone.

The square seemed empty. She stood for a moment admiring the stone facings of the houses set around it until the grinding of brakes and gears warned her that the bus, without waiting for passengers, was departing. She bit her lip, realizing that she had forgotten to ask how far it was to Malcarew, but a movement in the doorway of one of the houses caught her eye.

Two women stood together, watching

her with the wary, inquisitive look of sparrows. Helen disliked the way they huddled together, for all the world as if she intended some harm to them. Before she could clarify her impression, she raised her voice slightly, unconsciously adopting the slightly truculent tone of a woman who is ill-at-ease.

"Good morning! I'm looking for the house called *Malcarew*."

The younger of the two women came a few steps beyond the door.

"*Malcarew*? You cannot miss it. It overlooks the village."

She pointed beyond the square to the hill sloping gently upwards towards bush-crowned downs. Halfway up the hill, Helen could make out the outline of a house with tall chimneys.

"No more than ten or fifteen minutes' walk," the older of the women intoned, coming to stand beside her companion.

"I'm staying there," Helen said, wishing they would stop staring at her.

"You weren't expected until later," the younger woman began.

But the older one said hastily, as if to cover a blunder, "Any time is the right time to welcome a guest. Linton is a friendly village. The people here don't stand on ceremony."

Helen had opened her mouth to declare that she didn't know they were expecting her at all, but there was a shrill command from within the house and the two women hurried back into the shadow of the doorway.

As she picked up her suitcase again, the short hairs at the back of her neck prickled suddenly. She shivered, feeling the April wind break through the cocoon of sunshine in which the square was bathed. The place was not as deserted as she had thought. Three girls with arms linked went past her, smiling over their shoulders. A knot of men emerged from the public house at the corner and drifted away towards the stone houses. A dog ambled past, tongue lolling, and in the grocer's store opposite a couple of shadowy figures moved away from the window.

Helen set off across the cobbles, glad that she had travelled in flat heels. As she began to climb the narrow road winding up towards the house, a clock down in the square chimed twelve. At first the view was obscured by neat cottages, with, here and there, a larger dwelling set back from the road. There were several people working in the trim little gardens, and they all, without exception, bobbed their heads and smiled shyly as she trudged past. Obviously being a guest at *Malcarew* conferred some kind of social distinction.

The houses dwindled into patches of scrubland and then the road turned sharply almost at right angles and ended at iron gates, hospitably open, with the word *Malcarew* worked in scroll across both of them. Helen put down her case and stared at the green lawn and concrete path. There were a few flowering shrubs planted along the borders and late daffodils leaned out of the corners beneath a trim box-hedge.

The house was bigger than it had appeared from the village, a rectangular, two-storey building with a high, sloping roof. The windows were large and many-paned, glittering in the thin sunshine as if they had just been polished. Turning her head away for an instant, she glanced across the road, down past a sweep of cornfield behind the cottages. Every window at *Malcarew* looked down to the village, unobscured by trees or high buildings. No doubt the house, which could not be as much as a hundred years old, stood where the squire's dwelling had stood in the eighteenth century.

The breeze ruffled her neck again as she picked up the suitcase and went up the beautifully kept garden towards the gleaming white front door.

2

IT was stupid to hesitate before ringing the bell, but there was something inimical in those gleaming windows that stared so unblinkingly across the warm countryside. It was a modern, chiming bell pealing merrily within the silence of the house. Then, with no sound of advancing footsteps, the door opened and a girl with yellow hair tied back into a ponytail appeared on the threshold. She wore a dark blue overall over what appeared to be a black house dress with white collar and cuffs, but the severity of her outfit could not detract from the flowerlike prettiness of her face. At that moment she looked startled, flustered and excited, beginning to speak before Helen could put in a word.

"Oh, but you're very early, miss. I don't think we were expecting you today. They won't he back until one o'clock. I'm helping Gladys with the lunch now, so it'll be nice and hot. Oh, and me in my overall! Do please excuse it, miss, but I don't usually look so untidy. If you'll wait in the drawing-room, miss, I can bring you a nice cup of coffee, or would sherry suit you better?"

"Coffee would he fine." Helen managed to insert a sentence somewhere in the torrent of chatter. She was crossing a wide, thickly carpeted hall and being ushered into a room on the right. At the back of the hall a graceful staircase curved up to a landing beyond which an enormous stained-glass window reached up to the roof. Helen glimpsed the flicker of a skirt as somebody withdrew from the landing and then she was in a large, formally decorated room.

"I'm Sabina, miss," the pretty girl in the overall said. "I don't know if you've been told yet. Mr. Carew will be so upset when he finds you've arrived and there's nobody here to welcome you. Do make yourself comfortable."

The door closed and Helen, bewildered, stared round the white and gold apartment. It was hardly what she would have considered a comfortable room. The carpet was so thick that it made her feel sinful to walk on it, not a mark marred the tiny gold elephants parading along the shelves of the alcoves on each ride of the Adam fireplace. The thought of spilling coffee on the gold-brocaded chaos made her shudder, and the spindly-legged table was waiting to be scratched or tipped over.

Helen sat down gingerly on the extreme edge of a Louis Quinze settee and guiltily inspected the soles of her shoes, but they were clean and she blessed the habit instilled into her in childhood of automatically wiping her shoes as she entered a house. If the rest of Malcarew was like this she would never get through the day without breaking something. She could not imagine how Margaret, who had no feeling for beauty at all, could endure it.

There was a tap on the door and the pony-tailed girl re-entered, bearing a tray set out with coffee cup, cream jug, coffee pot and bowl. She put it down on the spindly-legged table, and gave an odd little bob.

"Please, miss, don't mind Tom if he

says anything. Gone terrible awkward has Tom."

Helen opened her mouth to ask who Tom might be, but Sabina had whisked back through the door. It was, Helen decided, rather like arriving on the stage in the middle of a play when one didn't know the plot or the other characters.

She drank the coffee reflectively and watched the diamond tipped hands of the small gold clock on the mantelshelf move slowly round.

A movement beyond the window made her look up, straight into the face of a young man in dungarees and checked shirt. He was staring into the room so closely that the tip of his nose pressed white against the glass. Then he stepped back a pace, still watching her in a cold, sullen fashion that was more objectionable than an open scowl.

There was the sound of a car in the drive and the youth swung away from the window and hurried out of sight. A moment later there were agitated voices in the hall and then the door opened and two people came in. Helen had a confused impression of a stooping, bespectacled man, and a thin young woman in a black coat-dress, with a fur toque perched on auburn hair, before the latter exclaimed in a high, well-bred voice.

"It was inexcusable of us to be out, but we never dreamed you would arrive before Patrick did. Or is he coming on later?"

"Hadn't you better perform the introductions before you start on the questions?" the man asked in a mildly complaining tone.

"Darling, how silly of me! This is my husband, Roland, and I'm Eve. But Patrick will have told you about us."

"I don't know Patrick," Helen said, flatly.

There was a brief, astonished pause, then the woman who had introduced herself as Eve said blankly, "But surely Patrick sent — you say you don't know him?"

"I came down to visit Margaret, Mrs. Carew," Helen said uncomfortably. "Just for a couple of days."

"Then who are you?" Eve asked in the

same blankly stupefied tone.

"Helen Clifford. I'm an old friend of Margaret's. She asked me to visit her, so I came," she finished lamely.

"Margaret asked you? Margaret?" the man called Roland said.

"I received a letter from her last Saturday. It's here somewhere." She had started to open her bag before she remembered that the letter was in her flat.

Eve began to talk very quickly, drawing Helen down to the couch and pulling off her fur toque.

"My dear, you must think our wits have gone wandering. Roland's brother, Patrick, is bringing his fiancée home some time this week. There was a possibility they might travel separately as Diana dislikes flying. I'm afraid we all naturally assumed you were she."

"I'm sorry but I'm not anybody's fiancée, merely a friend of Margaret's. Will she be here soon?"

"Here? But — oh Lord! You can't know, of course." Eve clapped a thin, heavily ringed hand to her mouth.

"Margaret is — is dead. We've just returned from the funeral."

"Dead! But she wrote to me last Friday!"

"She died some time during Friday night," Roland said, putting his fingers together and staring at the arch beneath them.

"But how? Was she ill?"

"It was an accident," Roland said. "One of those foolish, unnecessary accidents one can never foresee. She took an overdose of sleeping tablets."

"An overdose — ? Then wasn't it — ?"

"An accident," he repeated. "She was in the best of spirits last Friday. We'd just heard about Patrick's engagement, you see. We opened a bottle of champagne to celebrate."

"She took her usual sleeping tablet on top of the champagne," Eve continued. "We none of us thought of it at the time. I'm sure Margaret didn't."

"Apparently she woke up briefly during the night, forgot she had already taken a tablet and took another one. Normally it would have made no difference, but on top of the champagne — " Roland straightened his fingers, bringing the palms of his hands together.

"We'd told her not to keep the tablets in her bedside drawer, but she insisted it was more convenient there. She could take one with a glass of milk last thing at night," Eve said.

"Margaret never used to take sleeping tablets," Helen said.

"She began to take them just after Father died," Roland explained. "He was practically dying when they married, you know. She was more nurse than wife, I'm afraid, and those weeks were a terrible strain. Dr. Ferguson advised her to take something to help her to sleep."

"I see." Helen looked down at her own hands, surprised to find them trembling.

"My dear Miss Clifton, this must be a terrible shock for you," Roland said. "To come on a visit and discover such a tragedy!"

"Were you and Margaret very close?" Eve enquired.

"We were at training college together but we hadn't met for almost three years."

"But you wrote? You corresponded, you said." Eve's tone was politely interested.

"Occasionally. Postcards at Christmas."

"And she asked you to come down?" Eve's tone had sharpened almost imperceptibly.

"She suggested we might get together. As it happens, I have a week's free time and so I decided to come down. I should have written first, I suppose, but we were old friends, not on formal terms. And you're not on the telephone."

"Father hated them," Roland said. "He always declared that the telephone had ruined the art of letter-writing. It was foolish but he would never admit that he was a sick man, liable to need a doctor at any hour of the day or night."

"After his death," Eve said, "we often talked about having one installed, but you know how it is. We simply never got around to it."

Somewhere in the hall, a gong sounded. Its reverberations broke the slight tension which stretched between them.

"You'll stay for lunch at least, Miss

Clifton? Sabina has already laid an extra place."

"Eve, my love! We can at least give poor Margaret's friend a night's lodging," Roland cried.

"Why, yes, of course. Forgive us, but we're still a little shocked and upset."

"Of course."

They had not, she thought, looked particularly shocked or upset when they first walked in, merely surprised to find Patrick's fiancée there.

"You said Patrick was your brother," Helen prompted, as they left the drawing-room and passed into a dining-room furnished in opulent Victorian style.

"My younger brother. Let me take your coat. Do sit here. There's quite a draught from the hall sometimes."

"My husband fusses about draughts," Eve smiled.

"I was delicate as a child," Roland said, apologetically. "Patrick is six years my junior but he was always very hardy. A tough little boy."

"It's strange," Eve observed, "how all the strength and cleverness may he gathered in one member of a family.

33

Miss Clifton, will you have some smoked salmon? I am a positive glutton for it."

The serving dishes were of heavy silver, the tablecloth lace-edged. Her knife and fork were ivory handled, with a 'C' picked out on them in silver.

They ate steadily, Helen with questions still trembling on her tongue.

"It must have been a surprise when your father married again," she ventured.

"Oh, it was quite a romantic affair," Eve said gaily. "Roland and I were on the continent and Kate was here with her grandfather."

"Kate?"

"Kate is our daughter. She's just seven," said Roland. His voice had deepened and softened as he pronounced the name.

"She's at boarding school. There's more company of her own age there," Eve said, a shade quickly. "Unfortunately, she caught measles halfway through the summer term, and as she's a trifle chesty, it was decided to send her home. We were afraid she would be too much for the old gentleman, but he wrote and told us not to rush

34

back as they were having a splendid time together and he'd engaged a young woman to give her some holiday instruction."

"Margaret," said Helen, and the name sounded unfamiliar.

"They were married before we returned. Kate," said Roland, with the same fond intonation, "was bridesmaid."

"We were so afraid," said Eve, "that he'd been trapped by some awful gold-digger. But one couldn't help liking Margaret."

"A well-bred, intelligent young woman. She cared most efficiently for father." Roland sounded as if he were dictating a reference.

"But father grew rapidly worse. She took him to London to consult a specialist. Are you from London, Miss Clifton?" Eve leaned forward, fork poised over her salad.

"I teach at Surbiton. I've been given a few days off."

"In the middle of term? That's rather unusual, isn't it?"

"I haven't been — that's to say, I gave up most of the Easter holidays to coach some of the slow readers, so the week was owed to me."

She baulked at saying she had not been well. It was, in any event, not precisely the truth. Her small problems had reduced her to tears, but the news of Margaret's death had acted like a cold shower, bringing her to a sense of reality.

"I'm surprised Margaret didn't get in touch with you as she was so near," said Roland. "But then she was night and day at the hospital. In the end, he died very peacefully. Eve and I went up to join Margaret as soon as she wired."

"He passed away a few hours after we arrived," Eve said. "Margaret came back with us after the funeral."

"You lived here with her?"

"This is my home, Miss Clifton," Roland said, a tinge of reproach in his voice. "The Carews have owned most of the land about here for generations. My great-grandfather built the present house."

"Roland rides up and down pretending to be the gentleman farmer," Eve said with a bright, empty smile. "People in these parts have such mediaeval minds. The older ones are still apt to touch their forelocks and call him 'master'."

"The village seems very pretty," Helen said, lamely.

"I believe it grew up around the Carew family," said Roland. "Back in the seventeenth century there was a Linton Carew. The village was named after him."

"So terribly feudal!"

Eve yawned, touching her napkin to her lips.

"We'll have our coffee in the library," she said, a moment later. "After that you'll want to go upstairs and freshen up, I daresay. Perhaps this afternoon you'd like Roland to run you over to the cemetery. Of course, there's no permanent headstone yet, but we are making arrangements for one."

"My father was buried in London," Roland said.

"Oh?" Helen felt a faint surprise.

"You're imagining a family burial plot, with all the Carews tucked up together!" exclaimed Eve. "I think most of Roland's ancestors are buried up in the church, but for the past fifty years or so the old custom has died out. After all, it's living that matters, not where you lie afterwards."

"My mother was buried at Linton," Roland said.

"The first Mrs. Carew?"

"She died when Patrick was born," Eve said, leading the way across the hall to a room on the left. "The two boys had a nanny until they were old enough to go to school."

"Sabina's grandmother, as a matter of fact." Roland lowered his stooping frame into an armchair and motioned Eve to pour out the coffee. "Old Rebecca Grace must be in her nineties now. She was Rebecca Linton before she married. Her family go 'way back to the beginning of the village itself."

"And Sabina works here?"

Eve nodded, pouring cream with a liberal hand.

"Old Rebecca's daughter had an affair with some American. There's an air force camp over near Stansbury. It's been closed now but just after the war there were quite a few airmen hanging about, waiting for demobilisation. Anyway, Sabina is the result. Her mother ran off a few years later and Roland's father took the girl in."

"She's very pretty," Helen admitted.

"So was old Rebecca, I believe, though I don't remember it myself. These country women ripen early and are old hags by the time they're thirty," Roland observed.

"You're not from these parts, Mrs. Carew?"

"God forbid!" Eve exclaimed. "I spent my own childhood out in India. I was in Paris, wondering what the hell to do with myself next, when I met Patrick."

"Patrick?"

"My brother invited Eve to come over here on holiday, and that was how we met," Roland explained. "Ten years ago! It doesn't seem so long."

"Doesn't it, dear?" Eve smiled, eyes half-closed, through a haze of cigarette smoke.

"Did you like Margaret?" Helen asked, bluntly.

"Very much indeed," Roland said,

promptly. "She handled a delicate situation with great tact."

"Delicate?"

"My father-in-law left Margaret his entire estate," Eve said, coolly. "The house, the land, everything! She inherited it all, apart from a trust fund for Kate."

"But wasn't that unjust?" Helen asked, in amazement. "After all, his sons — "

"My father willed both of us a very generous allowance and stipulated that we should he allowed to remain at Malcarew if we so wished," Roland said in an expressionless tone.

"It was, as you see, a delicate situation," Eve said. "Margaret behaved very tactfully. She left the management of the farmlands in Roland's keeping and insisted upon dividing the profits between them. And she made no attempt to interfere with the running of the house. Sabina and Gladys manage it between them very efficiently."

"Gladys Jones is another of the village girls," Roland said. "And Mrs. Lewis comes up three times a week. We're lucky to get any staff at all during these days."

"I saw a young man in the garden," Helen remembered.

"Tom Weaver. He looks after the garden and does the odd jobs about the place. He's keen on Sabina," Eve said, carelessly. "Fortunately, Sabina has more sense than her mother had and keeps him firmly in his place."

Helen thought of the set, sullen glare with which the young man had surveyed her.

"I was wondering about Phoebe," she said.

"Phoebe?" Roland looked at her, questioning.

"Margaret mentioned somebody called Phoebe. I assumed she was a member of the family."

"Not of this family. I never heard of a Phoebe among the Carews."

"Perhaps it was someone down in the village," Helen suggested.

"Phoebe? Phoebe — there's old John Brewster's daughter at *Three Acres*."

"Her name's Penny," Eve said, impatiently. "Phoebe's an odd sort of name, isn't it? Are you sure it was Phoebe?"

41

"Quite sure. It was just a passing reference."

She spelled out the sentence in her mind.

'In this place only Phoebe is my friend.'

"Well, I can't imagine who it is. There's nobody in the village by that name. Anyway, Margaret didn't talk much to the Linton people. They're apt to resent outsiders."

"Perhaps it was somebody she met at Christmas-time. Margaret went to Switzerland just after Christmas," Eve suggested.

"She thought the change would do her good. I think she felt restless sometimes," said Roland.

"But she was happy here, you said."

"Enormously so," Eve assured her. "But she was sleeping badly and decided a little change would do her good. Patrick went over to Berne at the beginning of March and travelled home with her. We were pleased to be together again. Patrick and Margaret always hit it off together."

"Your brother doesn't live here?"

"Off and on. Patrick's the roving type. He enjoys travelling about and seeing the world."

"Isn't it strange," Eve observed, with the same sharp inflexion in her voice, "that the elder brother is always the one who stays at home while the younger goes out to conquer the world and win the fairy princess."

"And Patrick is bringing home his fairy princess," Roland said, without changing his expression. "He informs us that Diana is very beautiful. Of course he neglected to send a photograph."

"And we all assumed you were Diana, instead of which you came to see poor Margaret," Eve said, sadly.

"Poor Margaret!" Roland echoed.

Helen looked from one face to the other. So that was to be it! Margaret had become 'poor Margaret', to be buried and forgotten.

"I was wondering," Helen said mildly, "now that Margaret is dead, who will inherit the house."

"Really, Miss Clifton, I hardly think — " Roland began stiffly.

"Nonsense, it's a perfectly natural

question to ask," Eve interrupted. "The property reverts to Roland, of course. Margaret had no relatives, or so she said."

"She had none," Helen agreed.

"And we never heard her mention any friends," Eve went on. "She seemed so self-sufficient."

"Yes. Yes, she was."

Margaret had prided herself upon travelling light without emotional ties. Her last letter had been wrung out of the depths of fear.

"And it's a terrible thing for you to come to see her and find this," Roland was saying.

The library was warm and comfortable, furnished in brown, honey and gold. Books climbed up to the ceiling, spilled out into magazine racks. There were narcissi and dwarf tulips in bowls of beaten copper along the broad windowsill. Beyond the window green lawns sloped up to the white walled ridge of the downs.

"One would never think," Helen said, "that a funeral had taken place here this morning."

Roland flushed slightly.

"We don't go in much for drawn blinds and dirges in this family," Eve said lightly. "The dead are — dead."

"Please, Mrs. Carew?"

A light tap on the door and Sabina was there again, all curled pony-tail and smiles.

"What is it?"

"Mr. Ernest is here, Madam. He says he's come about Mrs. Carew's Will."

"Will? What Will?" Eve swung round and stared at the girl.

"Margaret didn't leave a Will," Roland began, and then, as if recollecting that he and his wife were not alone, he said briefly, "Ask Mr. Ernest to come in, Sabina. Ernest," he explained, turning back towards Helen, "is the family lawyer. He's young, unfortunately, but his senior partner died recently, and we hardly liked to take our affairs elsewhere."

"Mr. Ernest, Madam," Sabina said in what was evidently her best parlourmaid manner.

The stout young man in the dark suit bounced in on the soles of his neat, small feet, smiling broadly in a manner quite

45

unsuited to the occasion.

"Mr. Carew and Mrs. Carew! Fortunate to find you in! And this is Miss Helen Clifton, I presume? Come to look over your inheritance, have you? My, my, but what a wonderful friendship you and the late Mrs. Carew must have had!"

3

NOBODY spoke. If absolute silence existed, Helen thought wildly, then it must exist now, in these few, appalled seconds as they all three gazed at him, open-mouthed, incapable of comment. The lawyer was the first to break it.

"Oh, dear! Now I've revealed all. Do please forgive me, but seeing you already here I assumed — look, perhaps I'd better start at the beginning!"

"I think it might be as well," said Roland.

Eve said nothing but her face had a queer, greenish tinge. She had sunk down into her chair and was twisting the heavy rings on her fingers.

"I'm Paul Ernest," the young man taking a chair and lowering himself gingerly, smiled across the room to where Helen sat. "My father was the senior partner up to a few years ago. The firm was Ernest and Fenton then.

47

After Dad passed away, old Mr. Fenton took over the important business and I was kicked upstairs from law school to be junior partner. Then Mr. Fenton went into the land of the blessed, as they say, and I was landed with the baby, so to speak!"

"Must we have your entire life story?" Eve asked. "What is all this about Miss Clifton's inheritance?"

"I think I'd better read the Will."

The young man fumbled with the attache case he held on his lap.

"I think perhaps you'd better," Roland agreed. His voice was pleasant but there was something in his mild face that made Helen want to look away.

"Mrs. Carew — that is to say, the late Mrs. Carew — came in a week ago. She said she had made her Will and asked me to check it over and find two witnesses. My secretary and the cleaning woman signed their names, just under hers."

"And the Will? What does it say?"

That was Eve. How pointed her teeth were! And her nails were almost exactly the same shade as her short curly hair.

"I'll read it. It's quite short." Mr.

Ernest cleared his throat and read aloud in a precise, colourless voice, "'I, Margaret Carew, née Adams, do, being in my right mind and in full possession of my faculties — '"

"Just tell us what it says, without the trimmings," Eve snapped.

"It says — " Mr. Ernest ran his eye down the page. "It says, ah here we are! — 'do leave and bequeath all that of which I die possessed to Miss Helen Clifford, of 8, Terry Mansions Court, Surbiton, Surrey'."

"The property," Helen said faintly. "How much — is it a very great deal?"

"There's the house and contents," Mr. Ernest reflected, "and the four tenant farms, and that chunk of land over at White Meadows. Those are rented out of course, and most of the cottages are tied cottages. However, all in all, the property is worth — ooh, about two hundred and forty thousand pounds, give or take a pound or two. Then there are the gilt-edged securities — they bring in about ten thousand a year. Of course, death duties will be heavy, but even allowing for those, you should be certain of a living income of about fifteen thousand a year. The trust fund for Kate Carew and the allowances for the two Mr. Carews continue until their deaths and are separate."

"You're a very wealthy woman," Eve said, tightly. "What do you think of that, Miss Clifton?"

"It hardly seems worthwhile going back to school," Helen said, idiotically.

"Back to — I say, are you a schoolteacher? You don't look like the one I used to have."

Mr. Ernest regarded her approvingly.

"Can't you — didn't you think it strange that Mrs. Carew should have left all the money away from the family?" Roland asked.

"I did point it out, but Mrs. Carew reminded me that her late husband had done practically the same thing."

"But she was his *wife*!" Eve flamed suddenly. "She had some claim on him. Miss Clifton is only — " She broke off, but her eyes spoke the rest of the sentence.

"Mrs. Carew did mention," the young lawyer said diffidently, "that she was intending to make generous provision for you while she was alive. She intended to transfer part of her holdings towards you and Mr. Carew and Mr. Patrick Carew — a certain amount at the beginning of each month. The first transfer was to be on the first of next month."

"The first of next month?" questioned Eve. Then she began to laugh, folding her arms across her breasts and rocking to and fro in her chair. Her laughter sounded, Helen thought, listening almost dispassionately, more like screaming.

"Eve, please! Please!" Roland was on his feet, bending over her.

"I'm sorry, everybody." Her laughter stopped short and her voice sounded quite normal again. Only her eyes glinted bright and hard.

"It seems to have been a — a shock," Mr. Ernest understated desperately.

He had risen and was clutching the briefcase to him as if his life's savings were contained in it.

"Perhaps it would be better if you called back tomorrow?" Roland said, with an air of smoothing over the situation.

"Of course, of course." Mr. Ernest's

face was beetroot-coloured. "But there will be some papers for Miss Clifton to sign. I didn't bring them with me. Didn't intend to come over today, but it occurred to me it might be polite to give you a hint of what to expect. I was flummoxed, as you might say, to find out Miss Clifton was already here. Quite a coincidence it's turned out to be, your not knowing about this. My word, yes, quite a coincidence!"

Taking pity on him, Helen said, "I could come down to your office. Shall we say two o'clock tomorrow?"

"Splendid; fine. I'll see you tomorrow then. You'll want to digest this — yes, quite. I'll see myself out."

He stammered and flustered his way through the door, and Helen was left with the two of them. Roland had sat down again and was carefully polishing his spectacles. His eyes looked small and tired.

Eve said, as coolly as if her attack of hysteria had never occurred, "There must be something we can do. This is an intolerable situation."

"Patrick will be arriving any day. He'll

have to be told, and no doubt he'll think of something," Roland said, wearily.

"Why can't you think of something yourself for once?" Eve asked bitterly. "Why must it always be Patrick who decides? Can't you, for once in your miserable existence, make up your mind by yourself?"

"I think it might be best if I went up to my room now," Helen said, uncomfortably.

They looked at her as if they had forgotten her existence. Then Roland, with an obvious attempt to appear normally courteous, said, "We had thought you'd be comfortable in the green room, but now I suppose you'd prefer the master suite. Margaret used it but it can be tidied up."

"The green room will be fine. I'll find it myself. Sabina took my case up, I suppose?"

She hesitated, wondering what else could be said, but the two of them were staring at each other again, so she turned her unspoken sentence into a cough and let herself out into the hall.

The reality of her situation had scarcely

begun to penetrate. It was incredible that this large, beautifully furnished house should belong to her. And not only the house, but a big portion of the surrounding countryside and a sizeable income too. It was so incredible that, standing in the wide, magnificently proportioned hall, she almost laughed aloud. Almost, but not quite, because there was something indecent in the thought that all this was hers because Margaret had died.

Margaret must have known the family had a motive for murdering her and had sought to safeguard herself by willing her property to Helen. But, if that was right, why hadn't she told the Carews about the Will? Why had she gone on letting them believe the motive was still valid? And why think of murder? It had been an accident, hadn't it? A foolish, unforeseeable accident! One read about them in the newspapers all the time. People were always mixing up sleeping tablets and alcohol.

Or had it been suicide? A last, despairing gesture to escape — from what? Even as she posed the question,

Helen rejected it. Margaret had, in her own limited, practical way, enjoyed life. Her Will had been conceived and executed coldly and sanely, not out of fear but out of dislike of the Carews, though Margaret's sense of fair play had caused her to plan to make them a generous monthly allowance. Even if she had feared some harm to herself and had hit upon this scheme in order to keep alive, she had not thought of immediate danger else she would have told the Carews at once. Yet on the previous Friday she had written that panic-stricken letter, and on Friday night she had been killed. No, she had died accidently. It must have been an accident!

Helen began to mount the wide, curving staircase, her feet sinking into the soft, thick carpet. Her carpet now! And the golden elephants in the white and gold drawing-room, the ivory handled knives, the calf-bound books — they all belonged to Helen Clifton.

Had Margaret known this sense of unreality? Had she too stood here, looking down into the well of the hall, the semicircle of closed doors? Had she felt the sudden triumph of possession?

There was a movement behind Helen on the wide landing. She swung round, instinctively clutching the broad polished rail of the balustrade, and a butterfly, wakened from hibernation probably by the deceitful warmth of the day, fluttered across the stained glass windows. Up here there was a sense of space and airiness, a sense too of something to which Helen could put no name. A sense of — waiting? But it was not she herself who waited so sadly, so patiently. The very house seemed to be holding its breath.

She went with firm, deliberate steps across the landing and up a short flight of stairs to the upper hall which curved round a series of white painted doors. Her suitcase had been put in the green room, they said. Tentatively, she pushed open the first door.

It was obviously a staff bedroom and Helen, seeing the strip of worn carpet, the narrow iron railed bed, the gaudy print of the Good Shepherd, decided that part of her income would be used at once to improve the furnishings of the rooms not used by the family.

The next door opened into a small bathroom, the next into a larger room draped elaborately in lilac and redolent with the heavy perfume Eve had worn. Helen closed the door swiftly, unwilling to linger in the warm, sensual atmosphere which conjured up the presence of the red-haired, avid-lipped woman too vividly for comfort.

The next room was obviously the master suite. Standing on the threshold, Helen gazed in delight at the beautifully moulded ceiling, its cupids picked out in scarlet, turquoise and gold; at the white rugs spread over the polished floor; the wide white bed with its turquoise hangings. Then her brows drew together in a frown. Traces of the same heavy perfume hung in the air. She hesitated a moment and then went across to the window, pulling it up violently and letting the fresh, scentless air flow in. As she turned back into the room, her eye fell on the mink jacket tossed carelessly over the chair, the cut-glass bottles lining the dressing-table, the satin robe hanging at the back of the door. These were the accessories of a spoilt and beautiful woman. Margaret would never have worn them or used them.

An inner door opened and Sabina, a pile of fluffy towels over her arm, came in, stopping short as she noticed Helen.

"Please, miss, I put your case in the green room. Couldn't you find it then?"

Her voice was cordial but her blue eyes were sharp.

"You won't have heard yet," Helen said, ignoring the unfriendly look, "but Mrs. Carew has willed her property to me. That is what Mr. Ernest came to tell us."

"Left it to you? You mean, you own the house now?"

"That's right, Sabina."

"Well, I never!" Sabina stared open-mouthed, then her eyes narrowed slightly. "Will you be living here now then, miss? With Mr. and Mrs. Carew? And Mr. Patrick? Oh, whatever will Mr. Patrick say!"

"We'll find out when Mr. Patrick comes, I daresay," Helen said, patiently.

"Will you be wanting to use this room

now?" Sabina enquired. "I can move out Mrs. Carew's things."

"These are hers?"

"Mrs. Eve Carew's," Sabina said, blandly. "Mrs. Margaret's things were moved out on Sunday and Mrs. Eve told me to bring in her things from the lavender room."

Anger swelled up in Helen, directed, not against the girl who stood innocently awaiting instructions, but against the couple who could not even wait until the day of the funeral before moving into the main suite. All of Margaret's belongings had been swept away as if she had never existed.

"Will you be wanting this room?" Sabina asked, again.

"I'll move in within a day or two," Helen decided. "The green room will do for now."

"It's along here, miss."

Sabina opened the door again and led the way back along the hall to the first door.

"This is it, miss. I haven't unpacked yet. Will you excuse me, miss? I have to get on with my work now."

Obviously, she was bursting with the news she had just received, and longing to tell the rest of the staff. Helen nodded and went into the small room with the moss green carpet and the leaf-green hangings.

Her suitcase was on the floor by the low divan bed. Helen sat down in the swivel armchair near to the kidney-shaped dressing table, and stared bewildered at the white walls with their tracery of green boughs.

"But, surely — !" she began, aloud, and then, giving herself a mental shake, opened the door again, went out into the hall and stared at the semicircle of doors. The door leading into the green room was the first at the top of the short flight of stairs leading up from the lower landing.

She opened the next door and looked into a small, luxuriously appointed bathroom tiled in green and blue. Then the door next to it, leading into the lavender room. Then the master bedroom. Next to the master bedroom was a small apartment, intended, she guessed, to serve as a study for it contained a flat-topped desk, a leather chair, and two roll-topped bureaux. Next to that was a bedroom jauntily decorated in scarlet, then a broom cupboard, then a room sprigged in pink with a row of dolls sitting along the windowsill, then another small bedroom, then a room furnished in lemon and brown, then a larger room containing twin beds with pictures of pop-stars tacked up on a wall-board.

Eleven doors. She came back into the centre of the hall and counted them under her breath. Eleven doors, two of them leading into bathrooms, one into a broom cupboard, another into a study. Seven bedrooms, furnished in the same tasteful, expensive manner. Seven bedrooms, hung in varying colours — green, lavender, turquoise, scarlet, pink, lemon, and the blue room with the cut-outs tacked up which obviously belonged to Sabina and the servant called Gladys.

But the room with the iron bedstead, the worn strip of carpet, the gaudy print — where was it? The half-open doors gave no answer. But she had seen the room; had resolved to improve its appearance. She *had* seen it.

For an instant she had the impression that the thick carpet beneath her feet had wavered and rippled like grass. A new feeling was spreading through her veins. It took her a moment to recognize it as fear. Anxiety about Margaret, anger at the Carews, even startled excitement at her new-found wealth, these emotions were caught up and absorbed in a trembling panic that made her legs weak and her breath come short.

She went back into the green room and sat down again, pressing her hands together, stupidly enumerating in her mind the little, unimportant details of her life.

My name is Helen Clifton and I am twenty-five years old. I live at 8, Terry Mansions Court, Surbiton, Surrey. I teach at a junior school and for the past eighteen months I have been going out with Michael Barron who is an architect.

And less than fifteen minutes ago I opened a door and looked into a shabby little room which no longer exists. Less than fifteen minutes ago!

She rose, unwilling to sit any longer with no employment but her whirling thoughts, and lifted her suitcase on to the bed. In a day or two, she would move into the large bedroom with the gilded ceiling but this cool, green apartment was friendly. Strange that the word 'friendly' should come into her mind when this was the room that — but she wouldn't think about that.

She snapped the locks of her case and began to lift out her clothes. She had always had good taste but the few garments she had brought with her looked, she decided, exactly like the clothes a young, none-too-wealthy woman would choose. They hung forlornly in the big wardrobe above the shelf where she placed her slippers, another pair of flat heeled brogues, and the high heeled shoes she had slipped into the case at the last moment. She closed the wardrobe door with the resolve that she would buy some new dresses as soon as possible, and was confronted by her own reflection in the long glass on the wardrobe door.

It was peculiar, to catch sight of oneself

unexpectedly, to look at one's own image as if one were a stranger.

Mistress of Malcarew? Was this the owner of a large and handsome house backed by a substantial fortune? Helen stared intently at the tall girl in the glass. This girl had a face too broad and a mouth too large for beauty, her hair was pulled back severely from her face and the biscuit-coloured frock drained colour from cheeks already pale. Her figure looked too ripe for the virginity she still possessed, her hands were large. She met her own eyes, seeing them wide, blue, thickly hinged with short, blond-tipped lashes.

"I wish I could see what you're looking at," Michael had teased.

But she had only looked at what anybody else could see. The real world was there to be touched, smelled, examined with curious eyes. As to what might lie beyond — she had never passed beyond in order to know.

I do not see things that are not there, she told the girl in the mirror. I do not!

A memory crawled into her mind,

stayed there nagging at the security of conscious thought. She had been very small, small enough to look up at her mother as they went into a shop to buy some cakes for tea. Sticky buns with currants on their sugared tops — she could still see them on a paper doily in the window. But when they had walked into the shop, it wasn't a shop at all but a stuffy little parlour and a girl with bright red cheeks had sat coughing by a smoking fire.

The child Helen had drawn back, tugging at her mother's hand, frightened because there had been no depth to that little room and the girl had been thin as paper cut out and placed, coughing, by cardboard flames.

And then her mother's exasperated voice, "Do you or don't you want those buns for tea?"

And the shop again, bright and shiny, with a lady in a white overall reaching into the window and counting out the buns into a paper bag.

"Is the little girl all right? She looked very pale as you came in."

"She's been run down lately. Needs a

tonic, I think. I'd better have a loaf while I'm here."

Memory ended there, and her eyes questioned the eyes in the mirror. She had not thought of the incident again, had not remembered it until now. And she could not explain it nor fathom by what strange, subterranean process of subconscious association it had crept into her mind.

Helen went back to her suitcase, closing it firmly, lifting it from the green eiderdown and pushing it under the bed where its shabby, genteel appearance would not quarrel with the understated elegance of the room.

As she sat back on her heels, her eyes were drawn to a tear in the wallpaper just above her head. She got up and leaned over, seeing that what she had thought was a rip was simply the edge of the wallpaper roll coming away from the wall. It was loose all the way down and somebody had stuck sellotape along the flapping edge, no doubt until a more durable adhesive could be found. The bits of sellotape were drying and curling up at the edges.

Under the green and white wallpaper was a floral pattern. When she inserted her fingers in the crack, the two layers rose to reveal the plaster of the original wall. Somebody had written on the plaster with a black crayon. She could see the beginning of a word.

Helen pulled cautiously at the bits of sellotape, folding back the double layer of wallpaper, tearing it slightly as it came away from the plastered wall, from the wall on which somebody had written in tiny, clumsily formed, block capitals. POOR PHOEBE. POOR PHOEBE.

And that was all.

I don't know why They sent me here. I never wanted to come back. It was warm and quiet where I was before and nobody shouted at me. But They won't let you stay there forever, and before you can go on to the Other Place you have to come back. At least, that's how it is for me. I can't speak for anyone else. Although there were others there I never followed what they were saying very closely, and time was all mixed-up.

But when I found myself back here,

that was a bad time. The house hasn't changed, you see. Oh, there are grand new carpets on the floors, and you should just see my room, all green now, like the inside of a leaf. But the feeling here hasn't changed. It used to frighten me when I was little, feeling the air so heavy with hate that it pressed down on your shoulders like a beam of wood. When I found myself here again and the feeling not changed, then I was afraid and wanted to leave. Only there isn't anywhere to go. They made it clear that I was to stay in the house. If I don't, I'll never get to the Other Place.

I can't understand what I have to do here. I tried to talk to the Margaret woman, and in the end she was almost able to hear me, but by then it was too late because the dark shadow was over her. I don't know where she is now. They must have let her go on to the Other Place. Or she might be somewhere quite different. When I try to puzzle it out, my head gets in a muddle again and starts to ache. There are so many things I've forgotten, and there isn't time to learn them again, not with the Dancing day so near.

The Helen woman has become part of it. I saw her from the top of the stairs when she arrived and she brought something clean and pleasant into the house. But she can't stay here. I tried very hard and just for a minute I got inside her thoughts and she saw the room with my eyes, my yesterday eyes. But then she shut down her mind and I was outside it again.

I wish They would tell me what to do next. It's like the other time. I kept silent then, because I was afraid and not very clever. 'Poor Phoebe isn't very bright,' they said, and I wrote up POOR PHOBE with the black crayon Mr. Patrick gave me. But I let it all happen, and then I found out how to leave it behind and run away.

But I must have run round in a circle, because I'm back at the beginning again, and now there isn't anywhere to run.

4

IT was strange how morning altered the aspect of things. Helen, waking in an unfamiliar room, felt the clutch of apprehension dissolve into common sense as she saw her own possessions scattered about in the pleasant little room.

The rest of the previous day had passed more smoothly than she could have hoped. The Carews, evidently determined to behave well, had greeted her when she went downstairs again, if not with affection, at least with politeness. Eve had insisted upon taking her over the house, and introducing her to Gladys, a foolishly smiling girl with generations of inbreeding apparent in her rabbity teeth and pale eyes. Roland had brought out pictures of Kate who looked, Helen saw, like any other healthy seven-year-old.

The only note of discord had been sounded halfway through the evening when Roland, playing Gilbert and Sullivan records on a highly elaborate radiogram,

70

had commented, "This is Kate's favourite tune."

"You must look forward to her coming home for the holidays," Helen said, politely.

"She hasn't been home since father died," Roland answered. "She spent Christmas with a school friend and at Easter there was a school trip to France."

"Roland can't be bothered with children about the place," Eve said, carelessly. "He's quite lacking in the paternal spirit!"

"You know perfectly well that Kate could come home if — " Roland began, and then broke off, tight-lipped, and put on another record.

Kate could come home if — what? Helen wondered, but she was unable to complete the sentence. She was however quite certain that Roland loved his daughter. That had been apparent in his voice as he showed the snapshots of her.

Breakfast was laid in the dining-room. Roland, Sabina volunteered, had eaten early and gone out. Eve did not, it appeared, bother to rise until near noon. Helen, not displeased to be alone, enjoyed a meal she had not had to prepare herself and decided that Gladys, despite her stupidity, was an excellent cook. The previous night's dinner had also been delicious.

When she had finished, she went out into the trim garden. It had been, she thought, wandering round to the back, cleverly landscaped. Although it was not extensive, the lawns sloping up to the white wall, the twisting paths winding between the bushes, gave an impression of space. Obviously the sulky young man called Tom had been well trained and took a pride in his work.

As the thought crossed her mind, she heard a masculine voice, raised in anger, around a bend in the path.

"And I'm telling you I won't have it! I've heard talk and I'll not have it."

"*You'll* not have it?" That was Sabina's voice. "And who are you, Tom Weaver, to say what you'll have and not have? 'Tis only a bit of fun."

"Fun! Is that what you call — ?" The twig under Helen's foot cracked sharply

72

and she heard the swift patter of feet.

She walked on round the bend in time to catch a glimpse of Sabina's bobbing pony-tail. The young man in the checked shirt was flinging weeds into a wheelbarrow with great energy.

"Good morning. You're Tom Weaver, I believe." She had used the crisp no-nonsense tone occasionally in class and apparently it still worked, for he straightened up at once, wiping his grimy hands down the sides of his dungarees.

"Good morning, miss." His tone was respectful, his eyes wary.

"Has Sabina been telling you about the late Mrs. Carew's Will?"

"She said that the house belonged to you now, miss. Does that mean you'll be keeping on the staff?"

"If you continue to give satisfaction."

"Mrs. Margaret didn't have cause to complain," he muttered, with a momentary return to his former sullenness.

"Then I hope I won't have cause either. Are you walking out with Sabina?"

"I'd like to," he admitted, with a quick, shy grin that was not unattractive. "But she's flighty, that one."

"Most girls like a bit of — fun?" She chose the word carefully.

"It depends on the fun," Tom Weaver said, cautiously.

"You were very angry when I arrived yesterday," Helen said bluntly. "Why?"

"I thought you were Mr. Patrick's new fiancée," he muttered.

"But why should that make you angry?" Helen began, but he turned back silently to his work and Roland called from the path beyond.

"Good morning, Miss Clifton. Enjoying the sunshine?"

He looked, she thought, as if he would be more at home stooping over dusty volumes in a library than walking out in the fresh air. His rimless spectacles and neat grey suit gave him the donnish air of a man of fifty although she guessed him to be not much above forty years old.

"I have to go down to Mr. Ernest's office, I believe," Helen said, beginning to stroll beside him along the path. "I think I'll walk down to the village after lunch and see him then."

"Ernest has his office over at Stansbury," Roland said.

"Then I'll have to get the bus," she began.

"No need for that!" he exclaimed. "Can you drive a car?"

"I passed my test a few months ago," she said.

Michael had been so pleased that he had insisted on buying her a celebration dinner, and then had allowed her to drive his own car home, refraining heroically from wincing when she clashed the gears.

"Then you can take Eve's car. She seldom uses it. Eve dislikes driving."

"Won't she mind? I intend buying a car of my own soon."

She had been about to say that she would put down a deposit on a car, but now she supposed she could buy two at once, without noticing it.

"Eve won't mind. She didn't mean to be so — the news yesterday was a shock. To both of us. We'd thought — Margaret seemed to be happy with us. She never spoke of other friends."

"It must seem unfair," Helen agreed.

"We could find another house," Roland said. "The stipulation my father made about our staying here, I suppose that lapsed when Margaret died. You will have to ask Paul Ernest. He's not very astute, I'd say."

"And I'd agree." She felt a sudden burst of good fellowship towards him, because of the sunshine she supposed, or the thought of the money she could soon spend. Away from his wife, Roland was a nicer person, still prim and bookish but possessed, Helen thought, of a pleasant shyness.

"Why don't you come with me?" she asked on impulse. "I could buy some new clothes. I only came for a few days."

"There are some large shops in Stansbury," he agreed. "Take the car this morning if you like. But I don't think I'll come with you. There are so many things to be done." He looked vaguely round as if he were seeking employment. Then he said, eyes shifting uneasily behind his spectacles, "If you'll excuse me now, I'd better get back to the house. Eve will be — oh, the keys of the car! Here they are, Miss Clifton. You know the road to Stansbury?"

"I can follow the bus route," she assured him, and he nodded and hurried off as if he were glad to get away.

The big white garage at the side of the house was unlocked. She backed the car out cautiously and heaved a sigh of relief when she had negotiated it into the narrow road safely. It was longer and sleeker than Michael's car and her hands on the wheel were tense and clumsy. She was halfway down the lane before she remembered that her coat and handbag were still in her room. Obviously, the thought of money had gone to her head so badly that she was unable to perform the simplest action efficiently.

She drew up by the side of the lane and hurried back towards the house. The front door was open and Sabina was polishing the balustrade energetically as if she were still venting her temper on Tom Weaver.

"I'm going over to Stansbury. I won't be in for lunch," Helen paused to say, thinking how odd it seemed not to be walking into a crowded dining hall or rushing round the corner to buy something quick and tasty for lunch.

"Are you going in the car with Mr. Roland, miss?" Sabina stopped polishing long enough to ask.

"I'm driving myself in, if I can remember the road."

She ran up to the green room and delved in the wardrobe for her coat.

From the doorway Sabina said, "Please miss, could I have a word with you?"

"What is it?" Helen turned away from her image in the glass to face the girl who stood, duster in hand, confronting her.

"It's about — it's Tom Weaver, miss. You won't be keeping him on, will you?"

"Why not?"

"He's — he's a troublemaker, miss. Anybody can tell you that. He's not from Linton but over from Claymore way. Tom isn't popular, miss."

"I don't hire staff on the principles of popularity," Helen said coldly. "As long as he does his work well I see no reason for not keeping him on."

"It's not only that, miss." Sabina stood her ground, twisting the duster nervously between her fingers. "He follows me around all the time, wanting me to go out with him. And I don't want to go out with him, miss."

"Then tell him so," Helen said, impatiently. "Heavens, you're not a child, Sabina! You must be past twenty."

"I was twenty last month," the girl said.

"Then it's time you stopped acting like a schoolgirl!" Helen told her. "Now, if you'll excuse me!"

Halfway downstairs she paused, grimacing at her own prissiness. She was unconsciously becoming the type of sharp-tongued, unsympathetic schoolmistress she disliked; but there was something irritating in Sabina's shifting blue gaze.

She got back into the car and drove slowly down into the village square. The little town of Linton was as quiet as it had been upon the previous day. Yet she had the sense of eyes watching her from behind twitching curtains as she drove out on to the main road. The car was easy to handle, and apart from one unpleasant incident when a scarlet sports car roared past, causing her to swerve almost into the hedge, the drive was a pleasant one.

Stansbury was a larger more up-to-date place than Linton, boasting a cinema, a bingo hall and a short arcade of shops. Helen parked the car and, feeling slightly reckless at the thought of the sixty pounds holiday money in her bank account which could now be frittered on clothes, set off to explore, turning from force of habit into the large store rather than into the chic boutique at the corner.

By lunchtime she had acquired a misty blue mandarin-collared suit, a pair of bronze shoes with matching handbag, and a green and silver caftan which would, the salesgirl assured her, knock out her boy-friend's eyes.

"Only if he has to pay for it!" Helen retorted. "Will a cheque be all right? I'm staying over at Linton and I didn't come with any ready money. Mr. Paul Ernest can vouch for me, if you'd like to contact him."

"That's all right, madam, if you'll just put your name and permanent address on the back."

The girl bustled away to deck the clothes in striped grey paper. When she returned, she said, hesitating slightly, "Are you staying long at Linton? Until next month?"

"Probably. Why?"

"Oh, I just wondered. Not many people go to Linton — no industry, a bit off the beaten track. There's the last package, madam."

The girl smiled politely, but her mood of friendliness had gone. Helen thanked her and took the unwieldy parcels back to the car. There was a restaurant further down the arcade. She went in and ordered fish salad, eating it slowly to spin out the time until two o'clock. It occurred to her as she did so that she had filled up the day with little, trivial actions, as if to hold back the greater worries that lay at the back of her mind.

Mr. Ernest's office was in a side street of tall narrow houses. She needed only to ask the way once, and then was hurrying up dusty, uncarpeted stairs to the door with the brass plate at the top. It was flung open before she reached the threshold and Paul Ernest bounced in the opening.

"Saw you from the window, Miss Clifton. Come in, come in! Lovely day!"

Infuriatingly, endlessly cheerful, he ushered her into a large, comfortable room piled with books and stiflingly hot.

"My secretary's out having her hair fixed," he explained. "I should have remembered that you were coming and got her to stay in: but there's not much to be done. Proof of your identity, a couple of papers to sign, and then, unless the Will is contested, all should be plain sailing."

"Do you think they will contest it — the Carews, I mean?"

"I shouldn't imagine so. Both of old Mr. Carew's sons have generous allowances, and there's a large sum of money in trust for Kate Carew. There are no grounds for contesting the Will. Certainly they made no protests when the late Mrs. Carew inherited the property."

"They must have liked her," she suggested.

"They seemed to get on together very well," he considered. "Of course, I hardly ever saw the family. Mr. Fenton dealt with any matters arising out of the late Mr. Carew's estate. Mrs. Margaret Carew came in after Mr. Fenton's death and I saw her once or twice shopping in Stansbury, but I didn't see her again until she came in to make her Will."

"You didn't go to the funeral," she said.

"Toothache!" Mr. Ernest said succinctly. "I spent the whole of yesterday morning sat in a tipped-back chair having my gum pierced by myriads of needles. Then I went dashing up to *Malcarew*. Young Sabina told me Miss Clifton had arrived."

"And you assumed I already knew about the Will." Helen produced her driving licence and bank book for his inspection. "I came down to see Margaret. We were friends at college but it's three years since we met. I never imagined for a second that anything like this could happen."

"Like winning the pools, eh? Not that I ever try them. Have Mr. and Mrs. Carew said anything about leaving *Malcarew*?"

"The stipulation in the late Mr. Carew's Will ended, I suppose, when Margaret died?"

He nodded, and then asked, dropping his bantering tone, "What will you do about that? There have been Carews over at Linton for about five hundred years. They created the village, built it up from nothing, you might say."

"I think that we'll have to work out some sort of compromise," she said, uncertainly. "There is one thing. If I — if anything ever happened to me, the property would go to my next of kin, to my parents, wouldn't it?"

"Unless you left it to anybody else."

"I see. Thank you, Mr. Ernest." She rose and held out her hand. "Will you be coming out to *Malcarew* some time?"

"I don't go often to Linton," Mr. Ernest said cheerfully. "Linton folk regard Stansbury folk practically as foreigners, you know. Oh, if you want some immediate money, I can arrange to have a sum released. There's a sound little bank here in Stansbury. The Carew account is with it, I know, and I'd be happy to introduce you to the manager."

"You're very kind." On the threshold she hesitated and then said, "Does the name 'Phoebe' mean anything to you, Mr. Ernest?"

"'Phoebe'? Old fashioned kind of

name, don't you think? 'Phoebe'? Can't say it means anything. Is it important?"

"I don't suppose so. Margaret mentioned someone of that name in her letter."

She shook hands again and went briskly down the stairs.

The car was where she had left it, and as she slid in the clutch and felt the warm purring of the engine, the resolve to buy a similar car grew in her. It would be marvellous, she thought, if she could persuade Michael to help her choose it. She wondered suddenly if she would ever see Michael again, and then was astonished both by the thought and the sharp pang of misery it occasioned.

It had begun to drizzle by the time she arrived at *Malcarew*. She left the car in the drive and hurried through the light rain with her parcels, using her elbow to lean against the chiming bell.

There was a long pause before the door opened, and Helen, shaking raindrops from her bare head, looked into a flushed and smiling face, topped with thick blond hair. Blue eyes glinted with amusement at her dishevelled appearance, and a masculine voice said, "You must be

Helen Clifton. I'm Patrick, black sheep of the Carews. Please, come in."

"As the spider said to the fly?" she enquired, wanting to laugh at the ridiculous spectacle she must present.

"It seems to me that it's we poor Carews who are the flies!" he retorted, still smiling. "My brother has been telling me how we are all going to be flung out into the cold world."

"Not quite yet, I hope." Eve, wearing a loose fitting blue dress came out of the library and smiled with hard eyes. "Did you have any difficulty with the car, Miss Clifton? I was afraid it might be bigger than you could handle."

"She was doing very well when I passed her," Patrick said, lightly. "I was the maniac in the sports car, Miss Clifton. I wondered, after I'd passed, what a stranger was doing in Eve's car. Then when I arrived, I heard about Margaret."

"Were you sorry?" Helen asked bluntly, slipping off her coat and hanging it up.

"Not particularly," he said, coolly. "Margaret didn't approve of me and I found her something of a bore. Come into

86

the library and meet Diana. I persuaded her to fly home with me and she's still shaking."

He took Helen's arm and steered her firmly into the library. A very young girl was sitting by the fire and stood up as they went in. Helen's first impression of a shy schoolgirl was strengthened as Diana held out a narrow hand, and stammering slightly, "How do you do, Miss Clifton? I'm very pleased to meet you."

"Diana is an expert at saying the correct untruth," Patrick said, with gentle mockery. "Tell me, Helen, may I call you that? What do you think of Diana? Isn't she perfect?"

Perfect, Helen thought, exactly described the tiny figure with her hair tied in two golden bunches and her green eyes darkened by the emerald green dress she wore.

"Ooh, Patrick, you are awful!" Diana giggled suddenly, her hand to her mouth.

"And you, my precious, are very silly!" Patrick relinquished Helen's arm and leaned over to kiss the tip of his fiancée's nose.

"It hardly seems right to be enjoying

87

ourselves with Mrs. Carew — "

"Scarcely cold in her grave. What a conventional little soul you are, darling! I found her in Belgium, you know. She was stranded with no money and no idea what to do."

"It was this gentleman," Diana said, artlessly. "He engaged me to join a dancing troupe but when I got to Ostend it wasn't at all what I expected. We were all locked up in our rooms until the boat sailed, but I climbed out of the window and ran away. I was so frightened, not knowing the language and everything. And then Patrick found me."

"And lost my heart!" he exclaimed and Diana giggled again.

Helen was glad that Sabina came in then with the tea trolley. She could think of absolutely nothing to say that would have sounded even vaguely sensible, for one question filled her thoughts.

Why in the world had this handsome, elegant man chosen as a bride such a complete nitwit? Diana was certainly very lovely, but Helen had not been five minutes in her presence without discovering that she was empty-headed

and m
was a fa...
she had a s little common.
with her vowe... lity in her voic
could have done ...cceptible difficulty
this! ... Patrick Carew
... himself than
"You're very quiet," ...
her other side. "Are you alw... said on
or is this the result of the sho... silent
received?" ...ou've

"I don't chatter," Helen said, uncomfortably.

His hand brushed her shoulder.

"'Her voice was ever gentle and low; an excellent thing in woman,'" Patrick said.

"Cordelia," Eve said brightly.

"Is that somebody I've met?" Diana wanted to know.

"Cordelia, my love, is a girl in a play," Patrick said.

"Oh, an actress! I always thought I might make it on the stage," Diana confided. "But it's very hard to change over to legit. When one starts out as a dancer. And it seems rather a waste when one has long legs. Did you notice, Miss Clifton, that my legs are really quite long

though my body i
can be an adva
you in the fro
She gave
and licked
was holdi met Roland's bespectacled
Helen was sitting opposite them, in
gaze. of drinking a cup of tea, but
the cup was poised halfway to his lips
and the expression on his face was one
of complete and utter foreboding.

? Even that
cause they put
vapid little giggle
from the eclair she

5

THEY had settled down into what could, Helen thought ironically, be described as a pleasant family group. It would, she considered, be interesting when this artificial bonhomie began to crack. So far it had lasted for two days and most of the credit for keeping the atmosphere serene and lively had to go to Patrick.

He had established the pattern of treating Helen as a favoured guest who rather inconveniently happened to own the place. The others followed his lead more or less willingly. Eve seemed to be biting her tongue most of the time, but Roland had assumed a polite, avuncular air and Diana was innocently friendly.

Helen's first impression of her had been correct. The girl was foolish, badly educated, pathetically in love. Her eyes followed Patrick around the room and she hung on his every word, eager to agree with whatever he approved, and to frown at what displeased him.

Patrick treated Diana with the kind of mocking tenderness one might reserve for a troublesome kitten. It was certain that he did not love her. But why marry her then? Why burden himself with a girl who could offer only her inexperience as bait?

"I don't understand men at all," Helen said aloud, in her empty bedroom.

She had not moved into the main suite after all. The green room was a welcoming place, more welcoming than the other rooms. It was the sort of room in which one could say things aloud without feeling foolish.

Helen did not, in fact, find leisure to spend much time there. Patrick, having cast them all in the roles of happy family members, was determined they should play their parts convincingly and during the past two days had organized a visit to Margaret's grave with its fading wreath, an evening of home movies, a walk down to the village pub, and an evening of round games.

He had stood, bareheaded, by the newly turned earth in the cemetery and said, with the laughter gone from his eyes, "I told you that Margaret and I didn't get along too comfortably together, but it's tragic to think of her dying with all her life before her."

When they had sat in the semi-darkness to watch the flickering pictures, Patrick had provided a deft and amusing commentary on the antics of the child who threw a beach-ball towards her father, paddled in a rock pool, sucked candy floss as she squinted into the sunlight.

"Are all the pictures of Kate?" Helen asked, having hoped to see old Mr. Carew or Margaret.

"And they're two years old at that," said Patrick, "but we took her to Brighton that summer and I was being photographer royal at the time. We must take some more pictures when she comes home in the summer."

"You forget we may not be here then," Eve said.

"I don't believe that Helen will force you to leave until you've found somewhere to suit you," Patrick reproved. "She may wish to meet Kate. Even if you are a hardened schoolteacher, Helen, I defy you not to enjoy that niece of mine."

"Patrick is very fond of children," Eve said. "He is always begging us to send Kate to a local school."

"Kate is better at boarding school," Roland said. His voice in the gloom was flat and dull.

"But if we all wanted her at home," murmured Patrick, "wouldn't you consider the idea? Wouldn't you humour the whim of an indulgent uncle?"

"'Indulgent' is the right word," Eve said. "Patrick spoils Kate terribly."

"I hope he doesn't spoil our children," Diana said coyly. "I've already told him I want to have at least four."

Eve, rising to set her coffee cup on the table, stumbled and banged the saucer down clumsily.

The following morning, Patrick had rounded up the three women and marched them down to the village, declaring that he was not going to miss the chance of appearing in public with his three Graces.

It was astonishing, thought Helen, that

she should have imagined Linton to be sleepy and quiet before. It was buzzing with activity now; housewives bustling up and down, youngsters talking in groups, a knot of red-faced farmers discussing crops in the pine-panelled bar.

"I wondered," Helen remembered suddenly, "what they mean here by 'the dancing day'."

"The — what did you say?" Diana asked, wide-eyed.

"The dancing day. I wondered what it meant."

"Where did you hear the phrase?" Patrick asked. His voice had sharpened slightly.

"I don't know." Helen looked at him in bewilderment for an instant. "In a dream, I think," she said, slowly.

"Dancing day is the local village name for May Day," Patrick said. "You probably heard Sabina mention it. I believe she's entering the May Queen contest this year."

"A beauty contest? Oh, do tell us!" Diana clasped her hands.

"Eve knows more about it than I do. I wasn't here last year."

"About half a dozen of the prettiest girls in the village are judged by a panel of local villagers," Eve said. "The one chosen as Queen leads the dance around the Maypole. Later in the day, she and her maids-of-honour, the runners-up, have dinner at *Malcarew*. It's all rather boring really."

She spoke carefully as if she were repeating a lesson.

"My Lord," Patrick said suddenly, "but why don't you enter for it, Diana? You'd knock the rest of the competitors stone-cold, and it would save our having to entertain some bumpkin all evening."

"But would it be fair?" Diana was flustered and pleased. "After all, I'm not a local girl and I am engaged to you."

"The contestants needn't be local and I'm not one of the judges. Come on, Diana, promise me you'll enter. Eve! Eve, try and persuade her."

"It would please Patrick," Eve said. "It would be great fun for us all."

"Well, if you really think so — " Diana looked doubtfully from one to the other.

"Isn't anybody going to ask me to

enter this contest?" Helen asked, lightly.

"Would you like to?" Patrick turned glowing blue eyes towards her. "Oh, do say that you will!"

"Heavens, no! I was only joking. I never went in for a beauty contest in my life."

"That's a wicked waste." His hand reached across the table, rested briefly on her own and was withdrawn. "You would not languish unseen in a classroom if I had my way."

"I hardly languish in the company of thirty eight-year-olds," she said, laughing.

"I thought there was an age limit in these things," Diana pouted, tactlessly.

"Maidens only need apply," Eve chanted, raising her glass.

She looked, thought Helen, slightly drunk, her red hair curling about her small head, her eyes too bright, tiny beads of sweat along her upper lip.

Patrick evidently thought so too, for he put his own glass down.

"We'd better go up to the house now," he said briskly. "Sabina will have the lunch on the table. And Roland, if I know my brother's habits, will fidget himself to death if he has to eat alone."

As they came out into the sunlight again, Eve took Diana's hand and urged her on as if the prospect of lunch had just become unbearably tempting. Walking beside Patrick, she automatically measured her pace to his slow steps.

"I feel I ought to thank you for being so hospitable," she said. "You've made things much easier for me than they might have been. You could have resented me."

"Resented?" He looked up from his musings. "I suppose I did resent you, when I first heard the news. But you make that impossible. I enjoy your company and I appreciate your tact."

"My tact?"

"Don't you realize that by now you could have taken over the running of *Malcarew* and ordered us all to find alternative accommodation?" he asked.

"I wanted to — get to know Margaret's family better," she said.

"Margaret had no family," Patrick said. "She caught my father in a weak moment and married him for his money. My father married her and willed the property to her because he wanted to spite us."

"To spite you? You and Roland, do you mean?"

"He disliked us both. Some fathers do resent their sons, you know. Roland was nervous and timid when he was a child. Father bullied him and then despised him for yielding. He couldn't bully me, but he hated me because Mother died when I was born. It amused him to leave the property to Margaret."

"And did it amuse Margaret to leave it all to me?" Helen asked sharply.

"Margaret disliked us all," Patrick said gloomily. "She was always very polite, very correct, very distant. She was fond of Kate, I think. She went down to see her at school two or three times. But there was no open quarrel with the rest of us."

"And Phoebe? Did she get on well with Phoebe?"

"Who's Phoebe?" Patrick enquired.

"I thought I'd heard the name," she said, vaguely.

"Sounds like a maid in a mob cap," he commented, and she held a clear picture in her mind of a small, brown-haired girl with a cameo brooch fastening the collar of her grey dress.

"What do you think of my fiancée?" Patrick asked.

"Diana? She's — very pretty and very young."

"Nineteen, and I am thirty-six. You would not imagine a gay bachelor being caught by innocence and a prattling tongue, would you?"

"If his appetites were jaded, it might amuse him," Helen retorted.

"And what would you know of jaded appetites?" Patrick mocked gently. "What could you possibly guess of a life from which all spice of danger has fled, in a world from which all adventure has departed? What could you know of that?"

"Nothing, because I've never let myself get into that condition," she said, consciously prim, and felt a ridiculous pleasure when he laughed, not at her, but with her, warm and intimate.

"Perhaps I ought to come home to live," Patrick began, and then checked himself with a sideways glance, and a hasty, "I beg your pardon, but I forgot!"

"For the time being, at least, I hope

you'll continue to think of *Malcarew* as your home," Helen said quickly.

"You are indeed very kind."

As they paused at the gate, his eyes warmed, scanning the façade of the house.

"It's beautiful, isn't it?" he said, softly. "Did you realize that one has a bird's eye view of the whole village from the windows on this side of the building? And from every part of Linton the villagers can look up and see Malcarew. My great-grandfather planned it like that."

"He built the house?"

"There was a house on the site before, but it was small, and hidden by trees. Patrick Carew cut down the trees and demolished the house his own father had built."

"Patrick Carew," she mused.

"My namesake. He called his own son — that was my grand-father — Donald. That was my father's name."

"Why *Malcarew*?" Helen asked.

Patrick pushed open the door and smiled.

"My great-grandfather had a sardonic sense of humour. He had no wish to be regarded as what he was not."

"And he was evil?"

"Who knows what evil is?" he countered. "We may none of us find out. Shall we go in to lunch?"

She had gone upstairs after the meal, leaving them all to drink coffee in the dining-room. Throughout lunch, Eve had chattered without ceasing, her voice rising higher, her hands shaking almost uncontrollably as she poured water into her glass. Beside her, Roland hunched himself over his plate without looking at her.

It was a relief to sit quietly in the cool green apartment, away from the tensions that stretched between the family. Even Diana, for all her stupidity, had been aware of some undercurrent in the atmosphere. Her large green eyes had moved from one face to another, and she had grown more serious and silent as the meal progressed.

Helen took pen and writing paper from the drawer, and sat down, to send word to her school of the alteration in her circumstances. She would have to give a term's notice, but meanwhile it was only fair to let them know.

She wrote the address and the date and paused to rub a hand across her eyes. The drinks before lunch must have fuddled her brain. Her head ached slightly and the writing on the paper was blurred. She picked up the pen again, reaching out towards the inkwell. Usually she wrote things down with the pencil that Mr. Patrick had given her, but one must write in ink to a magistrate. Somebody must be told before the dancing day.

The badly spaced capitals zig-zagged across the page. Helen stared down at them, bewildered. What freak of the mind had caused her hand to move, spelling out,

'Dear Sir,
'I am scared. Come quick.'

She crumpled the paper in her hands and threw it almost violently towards the fireplace. There was no fire in the hearth, but the discreetly placed radiators were warm to the touch. The room itself was no longer cool but uncomfortably hot. There were beads of perspiration running down her face. She put up her hand to ease the tight collar from her throat and her fingers touched the shallow neckline of the linen dress she was wearing.

It was an effort to walk across the room, to push up the sash. But the air cleared her head and after a few seconds the tingling in her arms and legs faded.

There were voices on the path below her. She risked leaning out slightly and looked down at Sabina's yellow pony-tail and the thick, blond hair of Patrick Carew. The girl was speaking, so quickly that Helen could catch only muttered phrases.

" — cannot bear to wait! And we must get rid of — "

"Hush, love," said Patrick. His arm was about Sabina's shoulders and he bent as he spoke, to whisper further into her ear. After a moment, Sabina started to giggle.

Helen drew back as they began to move away. They were so deeply engrossed in their conversation that they had not heard her push up the window-sash. She wished she had heard more; something, anything! to explain what was happening.

But nothing is happening! Helen argued with herself. Margaret took an accidental overdose of sleeping pills. I have inherited the property.

But the Carews didn't know that Margaret had left a Will. They assumed the property would revert to them.

Even if Margaret's death was an accident, there are other things going on here — little, meaningless pieces that ought to fit together and don't.

Eve, switching so abruptly from blazing fury to a brittle, nervous friendliness. Roland, obviously loving his small daughter and equally obviously determined not to allow her to come home. Patrick, assured and sophisticated, with the naive Diana so much in love with him. Sabina, with her bright pony-tail and shallow, tinkling laugh.

But there were other pieces of the puzzle too, that ought to fit in but didn't. The name 'Phoebe' written on a wall, a room with an iron bedstead and a strip of torn matting, a memory of tight collars and sweeping skirts — she pulled back her wandering thoughts as her name was called from beyond the door.

"Miss Clifton! Roland would be very happy to go over the books with you, if you can spare an hour or two."

"Books?" Helen opened the door and looked down to where Eve stood on the landing.

"The accounts of the estate," Eve said, a trace of impatience in her voice. "Roland has managed everything since his father was first taken ill."

"Yes, certainly. I'll come down at once."

As she passed the other woman, she recoiled slightly from the sickly cloying perfume that Eve wore.

"I won't be bothering you this afternoon. Patrick is going riding with Diana and me. I don't suppose you ride at all, Miss Clifton?"

"I'll have to take lessons," Helen said, calmly friendly. "Perhaps Patrick can teach me, while he's staying here."

Without bothering to gauge the effect of her words, she went downstairs and found Roland in the library with documents spread over the table. He half-rose as she entered.

"The main bulk of the stuff is up in

the little study," he explained, "but these summaries will give you a clear picture. I administered the estate for Margaret and she was very satisfied, but you may wish to make other arrangements, of course. The accounts are all independently audited every year. They were done last at the end of March, and as you can see, everything is in order."

She heard Patrick's voice in the hall and then Diana's laughter. Then the front door slammed, and she went and sat down at the table, while Roland pulled up another chair and began to explain the intricacies of management.

By the time the others returned, flushed and talkative, from their ride, Helen was certain of one thing. Unless some fraud too subtle for detection had been perpetrated, Roland Carew was an honest man. He had increased the value of Margaret's fortune by judicious buying and selling. He bad kept the Carew properties in good repair and in parts of Linton the tenants were contracted to pay only a nominal rent.

"I take a pride in my figures," Roland said, as he clipped the documents together.

"I can see that you do. Margaret must have been very pleased with all this. She had a good business-sense herself."

"She didn't complain," he said briefly.

"Was she happy here?" Impulsively, she swivelled on her chair to face him. "Did she make any friends? Were *you* her friend?"

"She never complained," he said again. "But I saw very little of her. I assume she spent some of her time with Eve, but they didn't seek each other's company. Margaret spent quite a number of afternoons up in the green room, as a matter of fact."

"In the room where I'm sleeping?"

Roland nodded, unbending a little from his frosty impersonal manner.

"She used to go up there and read, I believe. Said the decor was peaceful. I would have thought her own room was bigger, but then the whole house was hers, so she had a perfect right to sit where she pleased."

He broke off as the others came in and Sabina followed with the tea trolley.

It was Patrick who shaped the rest of that evening. Beside his younger brother,

Roland shrank into a mild, scholastic blur against which Patrick's blue eyes and yellow hair blazed a defiant vitality. Beside Patrick, Diana was nothing more than a common little soubrette trying to ape her betters. Even Eve's red hair was tamed into limp ringlets clustering over her head and in the brief twilight her face was drained of colour, as if the flushed cheeks and sparkling eyes with which she had re-entered the house were no more than an illusion.

They had played round games until Roland, beaten on all points, had gone into the sitting-room to watch the news on television. Diana twittered after him, determined to be a sportsman even if she had won the last game. Helen, seeing Patrick's eyes rest on Eve's face excused herself, without knowing why she felt it desirable to go away.

Up in her room, the paper lay crumpled still on the floor. Helen picked it up and smoothed it out, willing the words to have changed; but the capitals leaped out from beneath the neatly written address.

'Dear Sir,
        'I am scared. Come quick.'

The window was still open and the air was colder now. She pulled down the sash and stood, irresolute, with the electric light sharpening the features of her reflection in the wardrobe mirror. Nothing in the room moved or stirred now, except herself. The room was empty of everything except her own fear. And she still could not put a name to the thing that lay in wait, could not reach out and grasp the pieces of the puzzle and mould them into a coherent whole.

Her arms ached from carrying the heavy buckets of coal up and down stairs and her hands were chafed and chapped from the long hours of scrubbing that marked washday. She was too tired to take off her dress and put on the white hand-me-down nightie with the little frill at the neck. So she kicked off her shoes and fell asleep, fully-clothed on the green canopied bed.

6

WHEN she woke up on the following morning, it was with a sense of well-being that surprised her. The strange muzziness of the previous night had vanished and she was clear-headed and full of energy. Sunshine was flooding every corner of the small room. Obviously she had forgotten to pull the curtains close the night before, though she remembered closing the window. After that she supposed she must have fallen asleep without bothering to disrobe for she was still in her dress, crumpled now after a night's rest.

It was late. As Helen glanced at her watch, she gave an exclamation of annoyance having neglected to wind it, but the clock downstairs chimed eleven. She opened the door and looked out into the passage. The other doors were closed, but she could hear Gladys's voice raised tunelessly in the hall below. In the bathroom, she stripped off her dress

111

and ran hot water extravagantly into the bath.

The new blue dress matched her eyes, and instead of pulling back her hair, she coiled it loosely on her neck. The first person she saw when she walked into the dining-room was Patrick, and he rose at once, complimenting her with a long, lingering look.

"I overslept," Helen said unnecessarily, accepting a cup of coffee.

"Overslept for what?" he inquired. "You have all the time in the world to do anything you please."

"Where are the others?"

"Eve and Diana went over to Stansbury, with Roland. I think my beloved fiancée is eager to spend her money."

"She's got mon — Oh, I beg your pardon, it's none of my business."

She drank her coffee, cheeks reddening in confusion.

"Perhaps I should have said *my* money," Patrick declared in an equable tone. "Diana's earning capacity is not exactly great. She graduated from fifth rate pantomime to a four grade strippers' club. But she's not tough enough, nor smart enough, to stand such a life. She's no family and no friends. Girls with her beauty don't find it easy to make friends."

"You haven't known her very long?"

"No more than a month or two." He moved impatiently as if the subject irritated him, and then said, apparently on impulse, "Why don't we skip lunch and get Sabina to pack up a picnic basket? We can walk up the downs — unless you have other plans?"

Helen shook her head. There were, she knew, several things that she could do. Certainly there were enquiries about the Carews to be made down in the village. But she might find out a little if she went with Patrick.

The morning was warmer than an April day had the right to be. They carried the large wicker basket between them, passing Tom Weaver who was weeding a flower border and grunted in lieu of greeting. "If you'll take some advice," Patrick remarked, as they began to ascend the slope of grass, "you'll get rid of Tom Weaver. He's from some town east of Stansbury. Been working here for only a few months. Apparently he's been bothering Sabina."

"She told me about it," Helen said. "But as long as he does his work, I see no reason to dismiss him."

"Old Jim Turvey used to do the garden. After he died, Roland engaged Weaver. It caused some bad feeling in the village."

"And in a close-knit community, etc. etc.? How feudal you are!"

"It was one of my ancestors who built up Linton," Patrick said, sharply.

"And ancestor worship is still practised in these parts? My parents will be amused when I tell them."

"Parents? Have you parents?" He paused in the act of helping her over the low wall.

"Did you think I was found under a gooseberry bush?" she enquired. "I have two parents, like most people."

"I didn't realize they were still alive," Patrick said, stiffly.

His face had altered; its lively, good-humoured expression hardening into dark and sombre bitterness. Then he laughed as if something very amusing had occurred to him and pointed across the grass.

"This is still free grazing land, until the planners decide to cover it with a rash of bungalows or cut a motorway through it," he told her. "We are still fairly isolated out here, but it can't last forever."

"Would you like it to last?"

"Why not? Don't you think it's a pity to destroy all the ancient traditions?" he countered. "There was a time when the Carews were an important family. Their word counted as law; as more than law, for they owned the land and the village, even the villagers, I daresay! As you say, it was all very feudal."

He went on talking, lightly and gaily, as they unpacked the basket. Almost against her will, she was drawn into his mood. As they ate she had to remind herself that she was not free to trust this man. The fact that he had been away at the time of Margaret's death meant nothing, for Helen had a vivid impression that Patrick kept his finger firmly in the Carew affairs.

But the sun was warm and the

surroundings pleasant. Despite herself, Helen relaxed, enjoying his company. Yet the tiny chill that crept over her when his hand brushed her arm was warning enough.

"You're very attractive," Patrick said suddenly. He was leaning slightly towards her and his eyes were intently blue. It was difficult to look away, difficult to recall that it was Michael she loved. She could not even adequately remember his face nor the words in which he conveyed affection. She tried to move slightly, to break through the langour that was stealing over her, draining away the energy with which she had begun the day.

But her eyes were closing and her mouth was pressed against hard, demanding lips. Then Patrick took his arms from around her shoulders and leaned back, watching her from beneath lowered lids.

"You shouldn't have done that," Helen said, shakily.

"Shall I apologize then?" His voice was mocking again. "Or shall I tell you the truth and say that, although I never intended it to happen, I'm glad that it did happen? I'm glad, because there are some women who can offer more than prettiness, more than charming prattle."

"You must have known many such women," Helen said, faintly.

"But they didn't all inherit the Carew estate?" he said, coolly.

"Did you try to make love to Margaret too?" she asked.

"She didn't attract me," Patrick told her. "Even if she'd inherited twice as much, she still wouldn't have attracted me. But you are — " He broke off, pulling tufts of grass with his long fingers. Then he finished, his voice lifting into gaiety. "You are a very comely creature. My great-grandfather would have appreciated you. He had an eye for what was termed 'a well-turned ankle and a pretty wit'."

"You talk as if you knew him."

"That's hardly possible as he died in eighteen-ninety. A man of forty with the appetites of a man of twenty and the constitution of a man of eighty. Death from excess!"

"How do you know all this?" Helen demanded.

"Our old nurse, Rebecca Linton, was

only about fourteen when Patrick Carew died. Get her in a lucid mood and she'll talk about Mr Patrick as if she expected him to walk through the door any moment. Shall we pack up the things and start back? The others will be home."

He was restless again, hurrying her to her feet as if he regretted the time they had wasted together. But as they were climbing over the low wall, he stopped abruptly.

"Diana is not quite what I expected her to be," he said. "If there was some way of breaking it off, without hurting her, would you be content to be a little more — closely involved? Because of the money, of course!"

His words were joking but by mentioning the attraction of her inheritance, he made it impossible for her to use it as a weapon against him. She acknowledged his subtlety with a smile which, she hoped, neither promised nor denied.

The long white car had just pulled up in the drive and Diana began chattering excitedly as soon as she caught sight of Patrick. Helen, guilt pricking her, waved her hand casually and ran through the open door into the house. Sabina, coming through from the kitchen quarters, asked in stiffly polite accents, if she'd had a nice time. Helen assured her the picnic had been delightful and went upstairs, wondering why Sabina's bright blue gaze made her uncomfortable.

Helen was brushing her hair when the sound of quarrelling voices rose and fell from the hall below. Eve and Patrick appeared to be shouting at each other.

"It's none of your damned business how I spend my time!" she heard Patrick say.

And then Eve's shrill and bitter voice.

"The rest of us dancing attendance."

And a giggle — that must be Diana — and high heels scraping sharply against the front step, and a door banging.

She put down the hairbrush and went out to the lower landing. There was no sign of Eve but Patrick and Diana were walking, arms entwined, into the library and Roland was leaning against the wall, looking, she thought, unutterably weary. As Helen began to descend the stairs, he straightened up, and assumed a tone in which shame and joviality were oddly mingled.

"Eve gets nervous these days. It makes her fly out at people. And she didn't like the idea of you and Patrick going off together. She thought Diana might be cross!"

"Isn't that for Diana to say?"

"I suppose so." Roland blinked nervously and then thrust out his hands. "But you know Eve!"

But I *don't* know Eve, Helen thought. I don't know any of you. Every time I think I have pinned down your characters, you move slightly, and the whole picture changes.

When she went into the library with Roland at her heels, Diana said, looking up from the depths of an armchair, "Eve thought Patrick had been neglecting me on your behalf. But I believe in leaving a man free, don't you? Men don't like to be tied down."

She offered the tired little cliche with a bright, placating air. There was a smugness in her expression that irritated Helen.

They had hardly sat down when Eve

came in again. Her tantrum was evidently over, for she began with an apology.

"I'm glad you're not holding sheer bad temper against me. It's going to Stansbury that puts me in a rotten mood."

"I'm exactly the same in an aeroplane," Diana contributed. "I really did intend to come on ahead by boat, but Patrick doesn't like me wandering about alone. He says I need to be cherished!"

"Patrick is right, my dear." Roland was being heavily avuncular.

"You travel a great deal, don't you?" Helen asked Patrick.

"A fair amount. I have business interests on the Continent." He sounded faintly bored but his eyes were wary.

"I've forgotten our surprise!" Eve exclaimed, clapping her hands in a poor imitation of girlish jollity.

"Surprise?"

"Well, it's more of an imposition than a surprise," Eve admitted. "But you have been expressing a wish to meet Kate. She's allowed one long weekend home every term if we choose. All the pupils are. So we wondered if we could bring

121

her back for two or three days next week. If we're leaving *Malcarew* sooner or later, I'd like to have her to stay."

"It's no imposition. By all means, bring Kate home." Helen said, slightly puzzled.

"Ah! but the question remains, who is going to fetch her?" Eve said archly. "She's too little to make the long journey alone, and Roland is too busy. I certainly can't drive all the way down to Cornwall and I wouldn't trust Patrick to get her home in one piece! We all know what a maniac Patrick is when he gets behind a wheel!"

"You'd like me to go down and collect her," Helen said, cutting through the tissue of flimsy excuses.

"Oh, would you? Would you really? It's too bad of us, landing you with such a responsibility. But I could drop a line to Kate's school and tell them you'll be picking her up on Friday next. Or, why not drive down on Friday and stay overnight? Then you could bring her back on Saturday."

"Fine," Helen said, pleasantly.

She glanced at Roland, waiting for an

objection, but he was folding a newspaper into a neat, bulky square and didn't look up.

After dinner, they settled down in a cosy, family group to watch a television play. Diana needed to have the plot explained to her at intervals and Roland took it upon himself to do so. Patrick had gone over to sit by Eve and the two of them leaned back, smoking and dropping an occasional comment into the pauses of dialogue. Watching them, Helen felt like an outsider. Before the end of the play, she was so bored and restless that she muttered some excuse about getting Sabina to make coffee, and slipped out.

It was dark in the hall. She stood for a moment, trying to locate the light switch and heard a creak from the landing above. Her first impulse to call out, 'Who's there?' was stifled by the instinct that whoever was coming downstairs had no desire to be seen.

It was Tom Weaver. She knew his outline as it trod silently across the hall, lifted the latch of the door, and was gone. He had been carrying his boots in his hand.

Helen let out her breath in a long sigh, feeling as relieved as if it was she who were the intruder. Then she walked firmly across the hall and pushed open the door leading to the kitchen quarters. The short passage ahead led to kitchen, larder, store cupboard and washhouse. She tapped at the kitchen door and opening it, heard Weaver's voice.

"Proof, I tell you! And you'd better listen!"

"Later, Tom. Come to the garage at twelve. Twelve sharp."

Sabina must have heard the click of the latch. Helen heard the back door close softly, and then the girl came down the long, raftered apartment, turning on an extra light as she came.

"I wondered if we could have some coffee now?" Helen asked.

"Yes, Miss Clifton. Shall I bring it in?"

"If you please. Was that Tom Weaver you were talking to, just now?"

"Yes, miss. He's after me to go out with him again. I'll bring the coffee in about ten minutes."

Helen smiled and closed the door again.

In the sitting-room, Patrick and Diana were sitting together now, while Eve gave them a criticism of the play they had just seen. She was standing up, talking animatedly, her hands weaving patterns.

"Sabina's bringing coffee," Helen said, going to sit by Roland.

"Good! Shall we have a brandy with it?"

Patrick jumped up interrupting Eve's flow and causing Diana to exclaim that she could never take spirits!

"I think I'll go up to bed," Roland said abruptly. "Are you coming up soon, Eve?"

"Sooner or later." Her glance relegated him to oblivion.

Helen drank her own coffee quickly, noticing the quick interchange of glances between Sabina and Patrick when the girl came in with the tray.

When Helen went up to her own room, she was too keyed-up to undress and so sat, fully clothed, with only the bedside lamp to dispel the shadows. She sat down and stared at her hands as if the lines on her palms were roads leading to the truth. But there were so many lines, so many tangled threads crossing and re-crossing in a pattern too intricate to disentangle.

She tried to work her way to the ends of some of them. Patrick was going to marry Diana but only that day he had made it clear that he didn't love her. He had also made it clear that Helen and the Carew property formed an attractive combination. If he married me, Helen thought, he would be able to continue living at Malcarew whenever he chose. He had been taken aback to learn that her parents were still alive. Because it made it useless to murder her? Margaret had had no relatives!

Helen rose and went over to the window, leaning her forehead against the glass. Her head throbbed as if all the thoughts and suspicions within were pressing against her brain. It was almost midnight. In a moment she would slip quietly out to the garage. There she might clear up at least one mystery.

As she waited, she became conscious of an indefinable change in the room, as if something unseen had entered and stood between her and the closed door. The cold was numbing her legs, forcing her to move away, pressing herself in the corner between bed and wall. Somewhere a clock chimed twelve. She must go now, leave the room, creep down the stairs and round the side of the house to the garage.

She must go, but she would have to walk through that icy cold to reach the door. She took a step forward and the cold swirled about her foot. In the centre of the cold something whimpered. She was not sure if she heard it or imagined she did, but she knew it was there, blocking the space between her and the door. The whimpering died; the cold ebbed away gradually and she was free — free to walk shakily across the room, to wrench at the handle of the door, to walk slowly down the stairs into the dim well of the hall, without looking back, without allowing herself to think.

Outside, it was dark and cold, with a faint sliver of moon throwing a sickle-shaped shadow across the path. The garage door was open but no sound came from within. Either Sabina and Tom Weaver had finished their conversation or they were late. She pushed the door wider and stepped inside. The shapes of the two cars made a deeper darkness within the gloom. At the back of the garage a ladder led up into the two-roomed flat where Weaver spent his free time.

Helen tensed, hearing the scraping of feet overhead. The feet moved cautiously and somebody, whether male or female she didn't know, was whispering. She could hear the syllables hissing down from above, and there was something indescribably horrible in the combination of the two sounds.

She backed away again and stood, hands clenched against panic, in the shadow beyond the door. Minutes passed and then from within the garage came the low whine of the sports car. A moment later it was backed out slowly into the drive.

Craning forward, she caught a brief glimpse of four figures huddled in the open car. Moonlight slanted across blond hair, whitened to silver, then the hood of the car was drawn slowly over the low-slung seats, and the car circled the drive and rolled into the lane.

Helen knew that she ought to go back

into the garage, explore the two rooms at the top of the ladder, but she was too terrified to do more than stumble back towards the house. Only when she had regained the silence and security of the green room, did the incongruity of it strike her.

The intense cold that had kept her prisoner was no more than a vague, intrusive memory in the warmth of the room. The sight of those four people leaning together in the moonlit car had frightened her more than anything she had ever experienced.

She shivered, reaching for her housecoat and wrapping it round her. She would have to wait now until the car returned. After a brief hesitation she turned out the remaining light and huddled on the bed, her ears pricked for the whine of an engine. Just before she slept, the clip-clop of hooves beneath the window roused her for a second. Mr. Patrick was riding home late from the village. Soon he would yell for the groom and stumble upstairs. Turning restlessly, Helen flung out her arm and forced the image of Michael into her dreaming mind.

Why does the Helen woman resist me? It's hard to creep into her mind when it's so full of thoughts and questions. Why can't she be still and let me do what has to be done? There is too much evil in this for her to fight. I have seen this evil before and last time I did nothing, because I was afraid. I am still afraid but the smell of fear is different now from where I stand.

If I could go outside the house, I might do more. But I cannot go outside except in another body.

I knew the man who works in the garden had crept up to Eve's room. He brought something away from the room but I can't explain what it was. I only knew there was evil in it, an evil I can't understand because things have changed since the yesterday time.

Mr. Patrick dresses differently and talks quickly. It's hard to follow everything he says but I know what he's thinking most of the time. It shows in his eyes, in the curl of his lip, and the way he moves his hands as if the riding crop were still between them. I felt that on my back more than once. I remember the sting of it.

But that was nothing then and it's less than nothing now. It was the other thing that mattered, the other thing I should have tried to stop.

Because I was a coward, the evil reached out and touched many others. And so I am here again to change it if I can. This Helen has a good brain if she will let me use it. The Diana girl is quite useless. She won't think until it's too late, until it's the dancing day and the fire is lit over at White Meadow and the torches are lit from the fire and they climb the hill to Malcarew.

It will be too late then. Too late!

7

IF I continue to sleep in my clothes, Helen thought ruefully, as she surveyed herself the next morning, then I may as well join a hippie community and be done with it!

She had not heard the car return but when she went into the dining-room they were all — even Eve — seated round the table.

Sabina came in with fresh coffee and Roland, unfolding a newspaper, commented that the political situation was getting worse.

Helen threw a stone into the pool of family contentment and sat back to watch the ripples.

"Did you see Tom Weaver last night, Sabina?" she enquired.

Sabina jumped slightly and a few drops of coffee spattered the tablecloth.

"I'm afraid Weaver has taken himself off in a huff," Patrick interposed. "Sabina showed him the door last night and he told her he wasn't staying around to be insulted."

"Doesn't he work on Sundays?" It occurred to her that she had not enquired when the servants were paid or the extent of their free time.

"He often goes off for the weekend," Eve said. "He'll probably turn up again tomorrow."

"Haven't you looked in his rooms?"

"Why? We don't have any reason to poke about in his things." Patrick raised his eyebrows slightly, implying a social *gaffe*.

"Would you like to go to church this morning?" Roland asked. "The rest of us don't bother but you're welcome to use the car."

Helen shook her head and said, as casually as she could, "I thought I heard a car last night just as I was going off to sleep."

"I went out for a spin," Patrick said, with a momentary hesitation.

"Oh, Patrick, how mean of you!" Diana pouted. "If you'd told me, I wouldn't have gone up to bed."

"Sweetheart, it was a sudden fancy. I

felt like a run in the fresh air."

"Well, I think it was mean of you," said Diana, pursing her lips into a kiss.

Eve said, sharply, "Patrick doesn't like to be followed around. Haven't you learned that yet?"

"I like to do the following," Patrick grinned. He was looking at Diana and something cold flickered at the back of his eyes.

"I think I'll take a stroll." Helen rose abruptly, pushing back her chair. "I suppose that Sunday is a very quiet day round here."

"Quiet as the grave," Roland said. "We usually sit around and read the papers."

"Then I'll see you later," Helen said, and went out quickly, avoiding questions.

There was a cold snap in the air unlike the previous day and the wind sweeping across from the downs was flavoured with rain. She hunched her shoulders and pulled up her collar as she turned into the lane. Her footsteps rang hollowly as she descended the hill, and as she passed the row of cottages, a curtain was twitched into place, a door closed quietly.

The market square was empty, save for a little boy aimlessly kicking a pebble.

"Can you tell me where Rebecca Linton lives?" Helen stopped and dangled a shilling before him.

He jerked his head towards one of the houses behind and grabbed the money before he resumed his solitary game.

The house, she noticed with quickening interest, was the one out of which the two women had stepped on the day she arrived. Its porch was shadowy, the door painted a dismal brown. Helen raised the knocker and tapped sharply.

Sooner than she had expected, she heard the drawing back of a bolt, and a woman with an apron tied round her waist, appeared in the narrow hallway.

"Good morning. I called to see Rebecca Linton," Helen began brightly, in the tone with which she usually interviewed parents on Open Day.

She expected unwelcoming suspicion but received instead a smile.

"You mean old Mrs. Grace? Linton was her name before she married, though everybody still calls her Rebecca Linton. Gets terrible fretted if people call her anything but Becky. You'll be Miss Clifton. Come in, do!"

Helen was ushered into a neat, musty room with a highly polished piano and framed Biblical texts upon the wall.

"Do sit down. I'm Lizzie Turvey. I live here with Becky."

"Turvey? Was it one of your relatives who used to be gardener at *Malcarew*?"

"That was my dad, Miss Clifton. He and Becky were cousins once or twice removed. After she was widowed, Becky made her home with us. I'm a widow myself now, these twelve months or so. My husband was a Turvey as well. You'll find most folks in Linton are related in one way or another. When you arrived we thought you were Mr. Patrick's fiancée. We were all curious to know what sort of lady he'd choose this time."

"The other engagement didn't work out, I believe." Helen wondered if her voice betrayed surprise.

"Apparently not, miss. A pretty young girl she was too. Why she was crowned as May Queen a few days after she arrived. And then to up and go like that without a word to anybody. Two years ago, it happened. Old Mr. Carew was away at the time on a health cruise and never got to meet her. And then last summer if he doesn't go and get married himself."

"You knew the late Mrs. Carew?"

"I saw her now and then but she wasn't the chatty type. Kept herself very close. Now, make yourself comfortable and I'll run and see if Becky is stirring. She's a wee bit drowsy sometimes in the mornings."

"Mr. Patrick's fiancée. Her name wasn't Phoebe, was it?"

"Phoebe? No, miss, it was Carla or some such name. Excuse me for a moment."

The woman withdrew and Helen was left alone with her thoughts. They were not pleasant ones. Indeed, they were so unpleasant that she shrank from following any of them to their conclusion.

There was the sound of voices and the shuffling of feet, and Lizzie Turvey came in again with an old lady at her side. Helen's first feeling was one of surprise. Having nerved herself to face an aged crone, it was a shock to see that Becky Linton, despite her years, still bore traces of the handsome girl she must have been. Her white hair was plentiful, her bent figure must once have been firm-fleshed and tall; her blue eyes were faded now but they looked shrewd and lucid enough.

"Now sit down, Becky, dear," Lizzie Turvey was saying coaxingly. "Miss Clifton from *Malcarew* has come down to see you. Isn't that kind of her? You'll take a cup of tea, Miss Clifton? I usually make one around this time."

Helen nodded, smiled, and waited until the woman had bustled out. Then she fixed her attention on the bowed figure in the neat blue dress.

"Becky? May I call you that? I've just come to live at *Malcarew*."

"Roland and Patrick live at *Malcarew*," the old lady said sharply.

"You were their nurse, weren't you?"

"I was their father's nurse," Rebecca said. "You wouldn't think I was ninety-four, would you?" she said, and sat back triumphantly.

"You look marvellous," Helen said sincerely.

"And so I ought. I don't drink and

138

I don't smoke and I never had but the one husband. Foolish creature *he* was! Walked out with me for seven years before he plucked up courage to propose and we'd not been married three years before he upped and got himself killed. Nineteen-seventeen that was, and me a widow with my Mary only eighteen months old! Hero indeed! Downright incompetent, if you ask me!"

"You went to *Malcarew* after your husband died?"

"I was born there," Rebecca said crossly. "I lived there until I got married. But I didn't go back right away after Henry, my husband, was killed. I'd a little home of my own, so why should I run back and wait on the Carews? Tell me that, eh?"

"You remember Mr. Patrick then? I mean, the first Mr. Patrick?"

"I was no more than fourteen when the master died," Rebecca nodded. "I was housemaid then."

"And Mr. Patrick had a son called Donald?"

"That's right." The old woman ticked off the information on her fingers. "Mr.

Patrick took a wife from over Heriot way. Can't recall her name but she was a poor thing, died when their son, Donald, was born. Then Mr. Donald grew up and married the vicar's daughter."

"And their son was Donald too?"

"That's right. Young Mr. Donald they called him. His father and mother were married at seventeen. I was his nurse."

"Until you married?"

"Bless you, no! I was twenty-two when young Mr. Donald was born. He went away to school when he was eight. I didn't bring Henry Grace up to the altar until I was nigh on thirty-eight years old. I nearly didn't have him in the end, for I was housekeeper by then. And three years later, he got himself killed!"

"And then you went back to *Malcarew*?"

"In a minute, in a minute. Don't rush me! Now, first old Mr. Donald and his wife died. Then young Mr. Donald got himself a wife. Ada Trent was her name. Mr. Roland was born, and then Mr. Patrick. That was when Mrs. Ada died, and young Mr. Donald he came down to me on the very night of her funeral. 'Becky,' he says, 'you'll have to come back to *Malcarew* and help take care of the child.' Well, I was nearly sixty then and I didn't feel like starting work again, but I went back. I thought it would be nice for my Mary to live up at *Malcarew*, but there! she was as stupid as her father. Wouldn't look at any of the local boys and then when she was past thirty she ran off with an American. It lasted just over a year, and then home she came with Sabina tucked under her arm. I was up at *Malcarew* still, so she left the baby with me and went off again. I haven't seen Mary since. I looked after Sabina until she was nearly ten. Then I decided to come down and live in the village again. Sabina stayed up at the big house. Young Mr. Donald was fond of her, and the two boys petted her. Spoilt her, I daresay, for I hear she's as choosy as her mother; as flighty as my mother."

"Your mother?" Helen caught eagerly at the last phrase, but the other woman was coming in with the tea.

"Sorry to have been so long but I was baking a few scones when you arrived, and they're nice and hot now. Would you fancy a nice, buttery scone, Becky dear?" She bent over the old lady who seemed to have fallen into a doze.

"They look delicious," Helen said, politely.

"You won't mind if I don't sit down with you, but I have to get on."

Lizzie Turvey set the things down on a side table and bustled out again. Helen began to pour the tea.

"I wasn't asleep," Rebecca said. "Just taking a little nap while Lizzie was around. Lizzie fusses!"

"You were telling me about your mother," Helen said.

"My mother? I never knew my mother. She ran away when I was a baby."

"But you were born at *Malcarew*?"

"My mother was a housemaid up at *Malcarew*. She was a Linton."

"And your father?"

"Oh, he died before I was born. My mother wasn't — wasn't married." For the first time, the old lady showed a trace of Victorian prudery.

"And your mother's name was — Phoebe?" Helen held her breath, as she waited for the answer.

Rebecca took a long, noisy gulp at

her tea and looked up vaguely. "Phoebe? Now, I've heard that name somewhere. Where was it?"

"Your mother's name — it must have been your mother's name."

"My mother's name was Sabina. I do know that because Mr. Patrick told me about her when I was a child."

"Told you what? What did Mr. Patrick tell you?"

But her tone had been too sharp. Wrinkled eyelids fluttered slyly and Rebecca folded her mouth.

"Roland was a nice little boy," she said suddenly. "Ever such a well behaved, pleasant child. But very timid and very careless with his pocket money."

"And Patrick? Was Patrick a nice little boy?"

"He's very good to me," Rebecca said. "Very kind to me. Very kind indeed."

"Like his great-grandfather," Helen asked. "The first Mr. Patrick, who told you about your mother, was he kind to you?"

"How should I remember that, after eighty years?" The old lady was visibly tiring. "Ask Patrick. He knows all about his great-grandfather. When I looked after him, he used to want to know all about his great-grandfather. I told him — "

"Told him what?"

But she had been too quick again. Rebecca closed her eyes stubbornly. Her head dropped heavily and she shrank down into her chair. Helen drank cooling tea, munched a scone, listening to the breathing of the old woman as it became deeper and heavier. Outside the lace curtained window it had begun to rain heavily.

The room was clean and neat and obviously used only for the occasional visitor. Helen put down her cup and went over to the small bookcase with the two Staffordshire dogs on top. If people were judged by their books, she reflected, then Rebecca Linton and Lizzie Turvey obviously never read any. There was a complete set of Dickens, with the pages uncut, a gardening manual, some recipe books, a pile of parish magazines and a fat, black Bible with blurred gold lettering on its spine.

Helen glanced back towards the snoring

figure in the chair, cautiously abstracted the volume and opened it. There were several blank pages before the table of contents was given. Most of them were filled with a list of names and dates. The word 'Carew' leapt out at her. Without pausing to think, Helen closed the book, thrust it deep into her pocket, and was back in her chair when the door opened and Lizzie Turvey came in.

"She seems to have fallen asleep," Helen said.

"Ah, she'll do that. Chat ever so bright and then out she'll go for a little nap. She's marvellous some days — clear as a bell, and then other days she'll get all muddled in her head and fancy things. Mr. Patrick doesn't like her to be bothered by too many visitors, but you're mistress at *Malcarew* now, aren't you? Do you like living there, miss?"

"Very much," Helen said, firmly.

"It's not a place I'd choose," Lizzie said. "Too big and staring, with all those windows. Shall I wake her up to say good-bye, miss?"

"No need. I must hurry for lunch. The scones were delicious."

She shook hands, smiled brightly to hide her consciousness of the weight dragging at her pocket, and was shown out into the rain. She ducked into it and hurried up the hill. Patrick opened the door for her.

"Did you see old Rebecca while you were wandering round the village?" he asked. "She's tough as an old boot, but her mind is failing very fast. Visitors tire her."

"She was asleep," Helen said, blandly.

"Well, you wouldn't get much sense out of her even if she were awake," he told her. "You'd better change your coat. It's soaking, and we can't have you catching cold!" His voice was teasingly possessive.

She changed quickly, thrusting the Bible into the drawer and ran down to lunch. It was disquieting to find them already seated as if they, being Carews, had the right to begin without her. Eve was in a fretful, complaining mood and Roland was being doggedly, persistently patient with her. Patrick devoted himself to Diana and passed only an occasional remark to Helen. Sabina, bringing in the dishes, looked sullen, drained of vitality, even her bright pony-tail hanging limp and dejected.

When the meal was over, Helen excused herself under the pretext of writing letters and went up to her room.

The Bible was an old one. It was almost impossible to decipher the faded brown marks penned, she guessed, by the Carews of the eighteenth century. She turned the pages, watching the ink become blacker and the handwriting less spidery. Then she found the name she was looking for, neatly marked with the dates of his birth and death.

'B. 1850. Patrick Linton Carew. D. 1890.'

Below this was the name of his wife.

'Jennifer Wharton. B. 1860. M. 1878. D. 1880.'

The cause of her death was recorded on the line beneath.

'B. 1880. Donald Patrick Carew. D. 1927.'

That was old Mr. Donald who had married the vicar's daughter when both were seventeen.

'Harriet Roland. B. 1880. M. 1897. D. 1926.'

And here was 'young Mr. Donald'.

'B. 1898. Donald Carew.'

The date of his death had not been filled in and there was no mention of his second marriage. But his first wife was there.

'Ada Trent. B. 1899. M. 1925. D. 1934.'

And below that were the names of her two sons.

'B. 1930. Roland Carew. B. 1934. Patrick Carew.'

Mentally, Helen completed the story.

Roland married Eve in 1960. Kate was born in 1963. His father married Margaret in 1969 and within twelve months both were dead — Donald Carew of old age, Margaret of an overdose of sleeping tablets. In 1968, Patrick brought home a fiancée named Carla, and in 1970 he brought home another fiancée called Diana. The child Kate was kept at boarding school in Cornwall at her father's insistence, though her uncle Patrick was apparently fond of her and eager to have her home.

Helen seized pencil and paper and wrote carefully, furrowing her brow as she tried to remember exactly what the old woman had said.

'Sabina Linton. B.? D.?
'Rebecca Linton. B. 1876. M. 1914.
Husband, Henry Grace, D. 1917.
'Mary Grace. B. 1916.
'Sabina Linton. B. 1950.'

Linton? Sabina called herself Linton, not Grace. But then she had been reared by her grandmother who had reverted to her maiden name after her widowhood.

She threw down the pencil and turning to the Bible rifled through its thin gilt-edged pages. Old Rebecca must have taken the book away with her when she went down to live in the village.

There was nothing else in the book, except a thin sheet of cardboard slipped like a bookmark nearly at the end of the New Testament. Helen turned it over and saw that it was, in fact, one of the memorial cards so beloved by the Victorians.

'Sacred to the Memory
of
Phoebe Linton.
B. 1860. D. 1878.'

The card was handwritten, edged in black. What made it so shocking were the gay little maypoles decorating the corners, their ribbons tied together in what was undoubtedly a hangman's noose. The delicate, cruel little drawing had about it something so unspeakably obscene that the card shook between her fingers.

Mr. Patrick had drawn it to amuse himself. She had a hazy memory of his telling her once that he might have been a great artist, if he had put his mind to it. He had drawled that he possessed hidden talents, like his ancestor.

But I can't remember such a thing, Helen thought, in panic. I can't remember something that happened after — after I was dead.

She turned back to the beginning of the book, running her finger down the faintly written names. It was difficult to make out more than the occasional line.

'B. 1720. Linton Carew. Died of Influenza. 1781.
'Frances Carew. B. and D. of the Measles. 1782.'

Apparently in earlier centuries it had been the custom to record the cause of death. Helen leafed back to the first page and studied the faint indentations. Her eyes were becoming accustomed to the old-fashioned script, but she had no clear idea what she was looking for. Only a phrase from a memory that

151

was not her own teased the edges of her understanding.

"Hidden talents like my ancestor."

And then quite suddenly she saw it, slanting across the thin page.

'B. 1700. Patrick Carew. Hanged for Murder 1730.'

Why had it not been scratched out, this blot on family respectability? That long ago Patrick must have been the father of the Linton Carew who had died of Influenza. Between their two entries was an almost indecipherable:

'Sa . . . Linton. B. 17 . . M. 1718. D. 1720.'

Why had the son let his father's name stand? Was it because Linton had loved him, remembered him? Or had the entry been written in hatred when a boy discovered the truth about his father's end? And had that hatred become twisted through the centuries to become a separate entity waiting to devour other members of the family? The evil in a man might possibly live on after him if it were strong. But would it live on for nearly three centuries or did it need from time to time to renew itself in the body and mind of another Carew?

From below, she heard Diana calling up the stairs that Sabina was bringing tea. The cheerful normality of the voice caused her to jump violently. Then she put the Bible back into her drawer and went slowly downstairs to join the family.

8

"**Y**OU won't forget that you're going to fetch Kate on Friday, will you?" Eve asked the following morning.

"It's remarkably generous of you," Patrick said, softening Eve's tartness.

"I enjoy driving and I like children," Helen said, mildly.

"It's still very good of you," Roland insisted. "And quite unnecessary to drag Kate all that way merely for a weekend. It unsettles the child."

"I trust I may be allowed to see my own daughter when I feel like it!" Eve snapped.

"If it were up to me, I would have dear little Kate home all the time," Patrick began silkily, but Diana interrupted with a sudden shriek.

"Oh, but you can't! You simply can't go to Cornwall on Friday!"

"Why not?" Helen looked at her in surprise.

154

"Because Friday is Mayday, the day of the beauty contest!" Diana cried. "I'm going to enter for it, don't you remember?"

"I doubt if Helen's life will be blighted because she doesn't see you parading in your best bib-and-tucker," Patrick said, lightly.

"But won't there be a maypole and side-shows and things?" Diana asked.

"You've seen too many amateur productions of *Merrie England*," Patrick grinned.

"You won't miss anything worthwhile," Eve said on a high, breathless note. "These affairs are terribly dull. We never even had one last year, and the year before wasn't exciting at all."

"Who won the contest then?" Diana asked the question that Helen was dying to frame.

"Car — " said Eve.

"Some village belle," said Patrick. "I'm not surprised that Eve can't remember. If I recall the occasion correctly, Roland had a drop too much and she spent most of the evening putting him to bed."

"Well, I think it's a pity," Diana said

sulkily. "Anyway, I shall certainly enjoy myself, even if I don't win."

"Oh, I've no doubt that you'll win," Roland said.

"And why not? Isn't she the prettiest thing you ever saw? Isn't she?"

Patrick put his arm about Diana's slim shoulders and looked a challenge at the others.

"Sabina is very pretty," Helen said. "She may give Diana a run for her money."

"Sabina is pretty," Patrick conceded, "but she lacks Diana's green eyes. Green eyes, like those of a cat."

"Sabina has blue eyes," Helen began, and the rest of the sentence formed itself in her mind. *Sabina has blue eyes like you, and yellow hair like you. And she has more than that. She has the narrow bones and elegance of a Carew. Sabina is a Carew!*

"I thought I'd borrow the car and go over to put some fresh flowers on Margaret's grave," Helen said, aloud.

"Rather you than me! I hate cemeteries," Diana shuddered.

"Take the car by all means," Eve said,

with an obvious attempt at friendliness. "We are going to have a long, lazy day."

"Then, if you'll excuse me." Helen nodded at them politely. At the door she turned, throwing out a casual question. "Has Tom Weaver turned up for work today?"

"Lord, I completely forgot to tell you. I went up to his flat over the garage this morning and it's cleared out. His clothes, shaving tackle, everything gone. It looks," said Patrick, "as if he took his marching orders from Sabina literally."

"I see." She met his eyes, pinned a rueful smile to her own face and said lightly, "Well, we'll have to find a new gardener pretty quickly, I suppose, before the weeds smother us all. I'll see you later on."

She wasted no time on the flat over the garage. If Patrick declared it to be cleared out, then she was quite sure that it would now contain no clues of any kind. And Tom Weaver had packed all his things and walked out with them in the middle of the night? Helen felt a sudden spasm of anger that they should think her stupid enough to believe that.

She drove slowly through the village and out to the Stansbury road, branching off when she reached the side road leading to the cemetery. She had not the faintest intention of spending any time at Margaret's grave, although she could have wandered freely round the entire place without comment. The only figures in sight were those of an old man leaning on a spade and talking to a taller man in a battered green trilby.

She manoeuvred the long white car past the low wall and stopped outside the grey-towered church. It was fortunately open, which saved her the trouble of seeking out the verger and saddling herself with a guide. As it was, she could wander quite freely round the dim building, with its high carved pews and unremarkable stained glass windows. There was nothing here to engage her attention, and she was trying the handle of the vestry door when there was a light step behind her on the stone floor. She swung round nervously to face a thin faced woman in a cheap cotton dress. The woman's voice was sharply suspicious.

"Can I help you?"

"Oh, I do hope so." Helen decided to adopt a conciliatory attitude. "I'm interested in old records of families and so on," she improvised. "I believe my own ancestors came from these parts and it would be rather marvellous to find out all about them."

She prayed silently that the woman was not from Linton, and her petition was evidently granted. The woman smiled and relaxed slightly.

"You'll not find any records here," she said. "We had a fire about four years ago. One of the choristers I daresay, trying his luck at smoking, though none of them would admit it. Anyway, it started in the vestry and nearly reached the main church. Mr. Walsh was very upset."

"The vicar?"

"Mr. Walsh was quite proud of our registers. We had them going back to the early seventeenth century. A history of all the families from all the villages around. Do you know where your relatives come from?"

"I believe one of them married somebody named Carew."

"Carew? Ah, they'd be the Carews from Linton. That's on the Stansbury road. I'm from Verney Cross myself. We don't have much to do with Linton folk."

"Not very friendly, are they?"

"They're very close. And there are odd tales about that place. I don't hold with 'em myself."

"Odd tales?"

"They used to say that Linton folk could fly," said the woman, scornfully. "All I know is that they give themselves airs."

"Do the Carews give themselves airs?"

"I don't know any of them personally. They're too rich to bother with me, but I understand they're still looked up to by Linton folk."

"I heard that one of them was hanged for murder once," Helen said.

It was almost too much to hope that the woman would know anything about it, but her eyes brightened.

"That was right back in the old days," she said, "in seventeen-something. Mr. Walsh told me all about it once, just after I'd gone to work for him. He was a real bad lot, that Patrick Carew. Killed a poor servant girl who worked for him. They say he used to entice girls up to the old house, and this particular one kicked up a fuss, so he strangled her. The villagers wouldn't have given him away, he'd such power over them. But the girl came from Market Greyston way and her brothers came over to Linton and found her lying there."

"And Patrick Carew was hanged?"

"In public, too!" the woman said with relish. "There were some folks who said he should have been burnt as a witch, but I reckon that was just talk."

Helen felt suddenly cold and sick; so dizzy that she almost mused the woman's next words.

"Funny, him being hanged, and then that other hanging."

"What other hanging?"

"Oh, some servant girl hanged herself over at the Carew house, close on a hundred years ago. A Linton girl, I believe. I don't know the story properly. In fact I don't suppose even Linton folk remember it. But Mr. Walsh is interested in these old records and now and then he comes up with some interesting story."

"Could I possibly see Mr. Walsh now?" Helen asked.

To her disappointment, the woman shook her head.

"He's gone away to visit his daughter-in-law at Cirencester," she explained. "I believe a visiting curate will be over next Sunday. Not that he need bother, for we don't get much of a congregation these days. It's very discouraging for Mr. Walsh. And he only left last night! Drove himself to the station at Stansbury. I don't expect him back for a couple of weeks."

"The church was unlocked."

"I keep the keys. There's no verger at present. I open up at ten in the morning and lock up at five o'clock. We have one or two nice brasses here and people sometimes come over to take rubbings. There's not much to steal. Mind you, we lock up at night now. We have done for the last two years."

"Why?"

"Some hooligans got into the church two years back," the woman said. "They stole a very nice communion cup and they left a dead cat, right on the steps of the altar. Such a nasty, wicked thing to do! Mr. Walsh was very upset about it. He called in the police, but they never found out who'd done it. It's lack of discipline. That's what's wrong with youngsters today."

"I'm sure you're right." Helen cut short the flow of words, and began the usual courtesies of farewell. Afterwards, she couldn't remember exactly what she had said. Under certain conditions, a person may act quite naturally even when the mind is reeling under shock.

She got back into the car and sat for a minute, her head bowed, her hands gripping the wheel. So the Patrick Carew who was hanged, had strangled a servant girl. And another servant girl had hanged herself when the second Patrick Carew had been master. And now another Patrick Carew lived at Linton.

Two years before, the communion cup had been taken from the church and a dead cat left in its place. Two years before, Patrick Carew had brought a fiancée to Linton. Carla something-or-other! And Carla had run away, like

Tom Weaver. But had they run away? Had they really run away? She knew the answer to the question but she couldn't phrase it. Instead she started up the engine of the car and drove slowly and carefully back to *Malcarew*.

Everybody was evidently out. The red sports car was not in the garage. Helen backed in the white car and then ran up the narrow steps to the two rooms over the garage. As she had expected there was nothing of interest in the bed-sitting room with its adjoining bathroom. The blankets were neatly folded on the divan bed and somebody had left a cup and saucer on the table. She peered into it hopefully but it was empty.

There was the sound of a car outside and, looking through the dormer window, she was in time to see the sports car sweep through the gates with Patrick at the wheel. She drew back hastily but he must have spotted her, for a few seconds later she heard him running up the stairs.

"Still trying to solve the case of the disappearing gardener?" he enquired, stepping into the low-ceilinged room.

"Well, the mystery is solved. Apparently somebody down in the village saw Weaver last night, hitching a lift on the Stansbury road. Asked him what he was doing, he was sick of being treated like dirt and intended to try his luck up north. So I reckon that's the last we'll see of him."

"I reckon it is," Helen said soberly. She was afraid to raise her eyes lest Patrick read the disbelief in them, but remained by the window, staring down into the drive. After a moment he came and stood behind her. She could feel his warm breath on her neck and, because the feeling was not altogether unpleasant, she moved away with a vague sense of betrayal.

"We will have to settle where you are all to live when I come back from Cornwall," she said quickly.

"Are you throwing us all out after all?" he asked, softly.

"No, of course not! But as the house belongs to me now, you will hardly want to remain here indefinitely."

"You credit us with a delicacy that we don't possess," Patrick remarked. "For myself, I spent most of my time

165

travelling, but Roland has lived here all his life. He has managed the property as if it were his own. He's an inoffensive fellow; even Eve can be bearable when she's not in one of her moods. Is it so terrible to have them here?"

"But they're not *my* family," Helen said in a burst of exasperation. "It doesn't seem to have occurred to anybody that I might want to get married and start a family of my own!"

"You're not engaged?" His eyes flew to her ringless hand.

"Almost!" she retorted defiantly.

"Then I needn't lose all hope." His tone was joking but his eyes were hard. "I meant what I said to you up on the downs."

"Diana — " she faltered, but he turned away impatiently.

"Diana is a fool," he said. "A very pretty, very sweet fool. I realized that the moment I brought her to *Malcarew*. Her helplessness attracted me, I think; but it was wrong to mistake pity for passion. That's why I'm glad you're going over to fetch Kate. It will give me time."

"To get rid of Diana?" She let her

voice convey only the surface meaning. "Why not do it now?"

"I can't just spring it on her," he objected. "Let her have her fun on May Day. She has never been, so she tells me, to a real country fair! I will tell her as kindly as I can as soon as the right moment comes. No sense at all in your involving yourself in unpleasantness."

"But I am involved!" she pointed out. "It is my house and my money."

"And you think that is all that attracts me? In the beginning, I'll admit it was true; and I'm not going to pretend that I feel passionately for you yet. I only know that every time we meet your money becomes less important and yourself more desirable."

He spoke with such rueful simplicity that she was almost tempted to believe him.

"You have money of your own," she reminded him. "Your father didn't cut you off entirely."

"I know that. Anyway, money is not too important, provided one doesn't have to work for it!" He gave her a quick, disarming grin which almost caught her off balance, and then went on, swift and serious, "But there is the house. It's been the Carew home for generations. The present house is built on the site of the house my great-great-grandfather lived in. There have been Carews at Linton for hundreds of years. And now, the house is given to — forgive me — a stranger."

"Isn't it rather drastic?" Helen asked, dryly. "Imagine marrying a woman simply because you wanted her house!"

"It does sound terrible," he admitted, with the same charming frankness. "But you forgot to mention that the woman in question is very, very lovely. I always admired ladies with golden tresses and dreamy blue eyes. And you're tall and statuesque, like some Nordic maiden."

His voice had dropped almost to a whisper and there was something hungry in his gaze.

"If you married me," she said, sharply, "you would be master of *Malcarew*. Wouldn't Roland dislike that?"

"Roland? Because he's the elder, you mean? I think he and Eve might enjoy living in a house of their own at

Linton, provided *Malcarew* was still in the family. He's a weak, amiable being is old Roland!"

"You despise him, don't you?"

"On the contrary," he informed her. "I'm very fond of Roland. He's been bullied all his life, of course, first by father, then by me. The only person who ever treated him with real kindness was Becky. She took care of us when we were children, you know."

"And told you about your great-grandfather?"

"He was something of a rake from all accounts. I must tell you about him some time," Patrick said easily. "Of course he died when Becky was fourteen, but he led many women a gay old dance before that. I imagine his wife must have found him a handful at times."

"Do you admire him?" she asked curiously.

"Of course I admire him," Patrick said, with a shade of impatience. "I admire any man with the sheer effrontery to live exactly as he wants to live, without regard for custom and convention. The Victorian age had room for its eccentrics.

Today we cramp them and confine them, force them into a mould of suburban respectability."

He stopped, shrugging and laughing, "In short, I'm an individualist and a traditionalist."

"And I am simply a teacher, dying for my lunch."

She held back from the temptation of matching his mood by allowing the spark of recklessness in her own nature to be inflamed by his rebellion.

It would be dangerous, she thought, as they went down to the house together, to under-estimate his charm, dangerous to ignore the fact that something in her responded to him. It would be even more foolish to forget that Margaret was dead and Weaver had vanished.

She turned her head and asked, "Was Margaret unhappy? Were you unkind to her?"

"I hardly knew her as a person," he said. "I talked to her; we travelled home from Switzerland together after her skiing holiday, but I can't claim to have known her at all. As I told you, she was a quiet, self-contained person who made my father happy for the last few months of his life."

Diana ran down the stairs as they entered the hall and threw her arms round Patrick in an eager, confiding way.

"Eve has a terrible headache and wants a headache powder," she said.

"I've got some in my room. I'd better go up and let her have one."

Patrick disengaged himself from his fiancée's adoring arms and sauntered upstairs.

"Roland is doing accounts in the library. I think he's making up the wages," Diana informed her. "I'm awfully glad that Patrick doesn't have all those dull things to do. But then the country is dull, isn't it? All that grass, and the people staring at one with their mouths open! And the shops are nothing, absolutely nothing!"

"If you'll excuse me."

Helen nodded to her and hurried into the library. Roland was at the table, counting out money into envelopes. He looked up as she came in, with a faint flush on his cheeks.

"The wages. I have authority to draw a cheque that will cover the wages, but Gladys and Sabina prefer to be paid weekly to save having to carry a lot of cash around. I don't know what arrangement you will want made after the first of the month," he said, awkwardly.

"I haven't decided yet." She went over and looked down at the envelopes. "You told me that Margaret signed cheques for the housekeeping bills but you paid the wages. Why was that?"

"Margaret had a passion for keeping the housekeeping bills down," Roland said wryly, "but the wages are regular. I'd always paid them in father's time so I carried on with the same routine."

"How much do I pay them?"

"The girls get seven pounds a week each, plus their keep. Mrs. Lewis usually comes three times a week to clean, but her daughter had a baby three weeks ago and she went down to London to help take care of her. Usually she gets two pounds for the day. Weaver got fourteen pounds a week."

"You pay out on Mondays?"

"If Weaver had waited until today before he took off, he could have walked out with fourteen pounds in his pocket," Roland said thoughtfully. "Funny that he didn't wait."

"Very funny," she agreed, taking up two of the envelopes. "Lunch is ready, I think. I'll give these to Sabina and Gladys."

"No need, no need. I'll take them in." Roland jumped up, but Helen was already near the door.

"I am surely capable of paying my own maids," she said wondering what had caused him to look so confused and upset.

Within the door leading to the kitchen quarters she paused to glance at the two envelopes marked in Roland's clerkly script. The one signed Gladys Jones was thin, but the one for Sabina Linton was bulky, too bulky for seven pound notes. The flap was only lightly gummed down. She slid her nail beneath it and a few seconds later was staring at twenty crisp five pound notes and seven single notes.

She slid them back, resealed the flap

and went through to the kitchen where the two girls were piling vegetables into the dishes.

"Your wages are here." She was proud of her calm, businesslike voice. "Don't be too long about lunch. I could eat everybody's share."

They gave her brief, smiling looks and slipped the envelopes into their apron pockets. If Sabina noticed the heaviness of her own she gave no sign, but a little smile puckered the corners of her mouth. It looked remarkably like the smirk of a girl who has just received payment for an extra duty well performed.

9

THE rest of the day passed without incident. Eve didn't put in an appearance for lunch, and afterwards the four remaining members of the party played cards, which whiled away the time without actually filling it. Diana played badly and Helen, who usually played well, was partnered with Roland who gazed at his hand vaguely and looked as if his thoughts were miles away. Patrick however was in his gayest mood. Once, Helen caught herself staring at him as she wished fervently that he could be trusted.

Eve came down for dinner, looking extremely elegant in a long-sleeved hostess gown of oyster pink. She was heavily made up, no doubt to hide the ravages of headache, and her hair was elaborately waved. Her eyes were feverish and she frequently rubbed her hands together as if she were cold. She ate, Helen noticed, scarcely anything at all, but constantly refilled her wine glass. Diana, sweetly pretty in a pale green dress, glanced nervously at the older woman as if she had scented a rival.

"I had a lovely, lovely sleep," Eve told them, smiling over the rim of her glass. "And then a long, long bath and here I am, risen from the waves like Aphrod — what was the woman's name?"

"Aphrodite," said Helen.

"Thank you, schoolteacher." Eve bowed gravely. "Aphrodite it is! What a super name. I wonder what she was doing under the waves."

"Eve, shall we go into the sitting-room and have coffee?" Roland asked, a pleading note in his voice.

"If the mistress of the house will allow it." Eve's voice was suddenly bitter, her painted mouth ugly. "We ought to consult her wishes for we're all living here rent free at her expense!"

"That's enough, Eve," Patrick said with a sharp edge to his voice. "You've had too much to drink."

"No, Patrick, dear. You, of all people should know that I am very far from being drunk," Eve said. Her voice was as clipped as his, her eyes hard, but as Patrick rose her hands twitched violently and setting down her glass she went meekly through to the sitting-room, her skirt trailing behind her.

"I don't feel well. I think I'd like to go to bed," Diana said, plaintively.

"Oh, for God's sake, don't you start!" Patrick said, with such savagery in voice and face that Helen felt a sudden thrill of disgust.

It evidently affected Diana in a different way, for she gave a pleased giggle.

"Isn't he masterful," she said. "I do like a man to be a man!"

"If you'll excuse me," Helen said, briskly, "I'll take a stroll in the garden. I have a busy day tomorrow."

"Busy?" Patrick looked at her enquiringly.

"Over in Stansbury," she said vaguely, deciding she was under no compulsion to give any of the Carews an account of her plans.

It was cold in the garden. She pulled her stole tightly about her shoulders and paced slowly, head bent, across the grass. It was impossible to make any sense of the scene she had just witnessed. Had Eve been affected by the considerable quantity of wine she had drunk or had her outburst meant something more? She had seemed to Helen to be teetering on the edge of a complete nervous collapse.

Helen paused, imagining she had heard something. She had been so deep in thought that she could not be sure that she had heard anything at all, but the noise, if it was an actual noise, had startled her, made her aware that she was some distance from the house and that there were deep shadows fanning out from the surrounding bushes.

She began to walk swiftly around the side of the house, stumbling a little over the rough turf. As she came round the corner by the garage she saw a light casting a narrow beam out of the half-open door.

The door creaked slightly as she pulled it wider. The two cars were still there, the one long and low, the other gleaming with hood pulled back. Above the sports car, the electric light bulb glared down on the figure in the checked shirt with cap pulled low over his face.

"Weaver? Tom Weaver?" She approached cautiously, her voice low and anxious.

The figure sat motionless, hands gripping the wheel. She moved to the side of the car, bent forward and tapped the figure with shrinking fingers. There was a curious rigidity beneath the check shirt, a complete absence of any sound except her own breathing. In sudden, blind panic she shoved the figure violently, saw it fall heavily across the gears, the head rolling loose on the floor of the car.

She backed away slowly, her hands to her mouth pressing back the screams that bubbled up in her throat. When she reached the door, she turned and ran towards the house, her legs shaking so uncontrollably that she had to concentrate upon each step she took to avoid being pitched forward on her face.

The front door was shut. She had closed it behind her when she came out. She raised her fists, beating them against the wood, forgetting completely that she needed only to press the bell.

The door opened and Sabina stared at

her in astonishment.

"Weaver! Tom Weaver!" Helen's voice emerged as a squeak.

"Whatever is it? Patrick! Patrick, something is wrong!" That was Diana, hurrying out of the sitting-room.

Helen had a confused impression of faces and voices; then she was sitting on the couch, retching as Patrick held a glass of brandy to her lips. The room came slowly into focus again and she began to shiver violently, pulling at her stole as it trailed from her shoulders.

"Helen, what is it? What's frightened you?" Roland was asking, in a shocked, concerned voice.

"Weaver! Tom Weaver is in the garage."

"But that's impossible!" Patrick exclaimed. "She's mistaken."

"He's in the garage," Helen said on a rising note.

"But you couldn't have seen him," said Sabina. "Tom Weaver left, Miss Clifton."

"I did see him! I touched him, but it wasn't him."

"Wasn't him?" Patrick repeated.

"His head came off," she said shakily, and began to giggle helplessly. "I pushed him and his head came off and rolled off the seat of the car. Like a — like a beach ball! It wasn't him, you see. I understand now that it was a dummy. A dummy in his clothes!"

Patrick was wrenching open the door and was running across the hall. Sabina and Roland had followed him.

"Drink some more brandy," Eve was urging. "You must have imagined it. God, but I thought I was the one who was accused of being tight."

She urged the brandy further under Helen's nose. The fumes made her head spin again and her eyes water. She put up her hand and pushed it away. Eve shrugged and drained the glass herself. She looked, Helen noticed with dull surprise, calmly amused.

Footsteps sounded and Patrick said, "There's nobody in the garage now. There's nothing there except the two cars."

"You're wrong!" Somehow Helen found the strength to get to her feet. "I saw him — *it*! In the sports car."

"Come and look for yourself," Roland invited.

She was too indignant to be afraid, but indignation turned to bewilderment when she reached the garage. As the others had said, the cars were empty.

"The light's on! It was on when I went in, and the door was open," she said, pointing up at the glaring bulb.

"The door was open and the light on when we arrived. Perhaps you opened it and switched on the light yourself," Patrick suggested.

"But why should I go into the garage at all?" Helen demanded.

"Well, why did you?" Patrick asked.

"Because I saw the light was on and I looked in to see if anybody was there, and he — it — was sitting there. I saw it!"

"And it was a dummy? But why should anybody dress up a dummy to look like Tom Weaver? We know he hitched a lift up north. It doesn't make sense," said Roland.

No, it didn't make sense. The Carews would scarcely try to frighten her away after the trouble they had taken to convince her that Tom Weaver had merely left.

"You must have imagined it," Patrick was saying. "The darkness often plays tricks with one's eyes, and we'd been talking about Weaver earlier on."

"But I don't imagine things," she said, confused.

Or did she? She thought of the unfamiliar memories that flitted into her conscious mind. Were they all simply a series of aberrations?

"Perhaps it was imagination," Helen said at last. "But it seemed so real. Like a — *so* real!"

"Nightmares often do." Patrick's voice couldn't have been kinder. "Waking ones must be the most unpleasant of all. You're white as a ghost and still shaking. Let's go back to the house. If I were you, I'd spend a day in bed tomorrow and go into Stansbury on Wednesday."

She protested that she was perfectly all right, but they surrounded her with attentions, pressing hot drinks and cigarettes upon her, telling her so often and so vehemently that everybody suffered similar experiences that she began almost to believe it.

She had not intended to remain in bed but she woke the following morning with a blinding headache that sent pain stabbing behind her eyes when she moved her head.

Diana tapped on the door at mid-morning, carrying tea and toast, and full of concern for Helen's white face and heavy eyes.

"I'd stay and keep you company," she offered, "but we're going to Carnston for the day. There are some wedding rings there and Patrick wants me to choose one. He says that he'd like us to be married as soon as possible. Would you let us be married from here? I don't have any relatives."

"Yes, of course. Anything you say." Helen closed her eyes against the tea and toast and thankfully heard Diana tiptoe away.

The sound of the returning car woke her late in the afternoon. Her headache had gone and she felt ravenously hungry. She dressed carefully, putting on the new caftan and twisting her hair into a Grecian knot. As she put the final coating of mascara on her lashes, she thought suddenly of Michael who had often admired that particular hair-style. If only he were here at Malcarew! She had written to him telling him briefly of Margaret's death and of her inheritance, and promising she would be back at the end of the week. It would have been so easy to send a second letter begging him to come down, but a few moments' thought had convinced her that to do so would be useless. They would find some way of getting rid of him by the first of May. She was not certain exactly whom she meant by 'they'. Patrick certainly, and Sabina, probably Eve, and Roland? She couldn't make up her mind about Roland.

When she walked into the dining-room, it was Roland who jumped up to pull out her chair and enquire anxiously if she felt better.

"Much better, thank you. I can't remember having such a headache before."

"You had a nasty experience," Diana began, but Patrick interrupted sharply.

"We agreed not to mention last night!"

"Did you find a wedding ring that

185

pleased you?" Helen asked.

"Oh, there were so many!" Diana clasped her hands rapturously. "I never saw so many pretty rings in my whole life. I just couldn't make up my mind, could I, darling?"

"That's an understatement," Patrick said, heartily. "She must have looked at more than fifty, Helen, and she still couldn't decide."

"I didn't know if I wanted a plain band or one with little stones all round it. Do you think that would be too gaudy?"

Helen mumbled something non-committal as she ate the cold duckling and salad on her plate. There was something horrible in the gaiety with which Diana chattered about her marriage, for it was obvious that Patrick had not the faintest intention of marrying her. Anybody but a fool could have interpreted his sardonic smile and faintly lifted eyebrow.

Eve was nervous again. There were dark shadows under her eyes and the bones of her skull seemed to be pressing against her skin. She kept wiping the palms of her hands against her napkin

186

and licking her lips. Now and then she cast quick, frightened glances towards Patrick.

Sabina brought in a dish of peaches.

"Are you feeling better, Miss Clifton?" she asked, tones dripping honey, as she set the dessert on the table.

Looking at her, Helen disliked the smooth pink and white cheeks, shallow blue eyes and smiling lips. There was something in the servant that reminded her of a mechanical doll she had once seen that bobbed a series of curtseys when one turned a key in its back.

"It was a headache I had," she said sharply. "There's no need to treat me as if I were just recovering from the plague!"

"I'm sorry, miss, I'm sure," the girl said stiffly.

"Miss Clifton isn't feeling quite herself," said Patrick in a quiet, sickroom voice.

"I was never more myself," Helen said flatly.

She was tired of being told how she felt, tired of being led, as if blindfolded, from one situation to another.

"Whatever you may think," she said,

defiantly, "I know what I saw last night. I touched it, pushed it; and you can't pretend that it didn't happen by refusing to talk about it."

"Somebody played a joke then?" Diana suggested.

"Why would anybody do such a thing?" Patrick asked reasonably.

To frighten me, Helen thought suddenly. To frighten me away from this house. But in that case why did Patrick attempt to make love to her?

"Where were you last night, Patrick, when I was in the garden?" she asked.

"In the sitting-room, drinking coffee," he said, in a faint tone of surprise.

"No, you weren't, darling," Diana said. "You went through to the kitchen to get some of those coloured sugar crystals I said I liked."

"Roland?"

"I went upstairs to wash my hands," Roland said. "And I must say that I do rather resent the implications of your question!"

"Eve? Where were you?"

"In the sitting-room, talking to Diana; and I never moved from there until you

188

came banging at the front door. And I resent being questioned too," Eve said shrilly. "I certainly never went anywhere near the garage. I wouldn't play such a terrible joke on anybody."

"Then, if I'm wrong, I apologize," Helen said, unwillingly.

"You talk as if we'd made you unwelcome," said Roland. "It's not easy for us to see our family home pass into strange hands, you know. We could have tried to upset the Will when father died, but we agreed that it was best not to make a fuss."

"I think it might be an excellent idea if we drifted into the sitting-room now and had our coffee," Patrick remarked. "There is nothing more sordid than a family quarrel. For my own part, I'm quite prepared to accept that somebody played a stupid and rather horrifying joke. If I find out that it was one of us, I'll be angry. I won't say more than that. As for the other matter, I'm sure that we'll get precisely nowhere by raking up who owns what and so on. It's highly embarrassing for Diana and Helen, and highly unprofitable for the rest of us!"

"Then do let us talk about something pleasant," Diana begged. "We had a lovely time today, Helen. Roland took me to the cinema this afternoon. There are two cinemas at Carnston, and we went to see the Elizabeth Taylor film. I do admire her looks, don't you?"

"Didn't Eve and Patrick see the film?"

"Eve had seen it before and Patrick had some business in town, so we met up later and drove back together," Roland explained, a shade too punctiliously.

"I see," said Helen.

But she didn't see. These stray comings and goings were confusing her. There was no reason in the world why the four of them shouldn't have gone off that morning to look at wedding rings, separated and met up again later. There was no reason why she should not have had a headache that day which prevented her from going into Stansbury, except that she was not usually subject to headaches and doubted if even the fright she had received could have produced one.

She had drunk brandy after running in from the garage, but then Eve had finished off the glass and was not complaining of headache. But at dinner time, there had been two carafes of wine. Helen herself had taken a glass of white wine; the others — what had they drunk? She couldn't remember the colour of the liquid in their goblets, except for Eve's. Eve had drunk red wine.

To distract her thoughts, she picked up a magazine and leafed through it idly. The bright, glossy pictures of fashion models looked so normal, so far removed from the atmosphere of terror in which she was trapped. And yet she had only to walk out of the house, go to the nearest police station and tell them — what?

My friend has died suddenly after appealing to me for help. The gardener walked out and left his wages behind, and somebody put a dummy in the car to frighten me. Two years ago a communion cup was stolen and a dead cat left on the altar steps of the church. Two years ago, Patrick Carew's fiancée was crowned as May Queen in Linton. Two years ago his fiancée went off without a word.

She could imagine the politely humouring looks, the soothing patter.

"So you were given a week's leave

because the headmistress thought you tired and nervous. You went down to stay with an old friend and discovered on arrival that she was dead and had left all her property to you. That must have been a nasty shock, Miss Clifton. Could even have knocked you off balance a little, made you a trifle fanciful."

She threw down the magazine and looked up, meeting Diana's green eyes. There was a coldly considering look in them so unlike the usual wide innocence.

"What's the matter?"

"What should be the matter?" Diana asked, leaning back in the armchair and yawning.

"Nothing. I thought you were going to say something. Where are the others?" She was not aware the Carews had left the room.

"They wandered off. Patrick is going round the garden and garage to make sure everything is locked up. You like Patrick, don't you?"

"He's very charming," Helen evaded.

"But you're almost engaged, aren't you?" Diana persisted.

So that had been the reason for the

coldly considering look. Diana feared a rival for Patrick's affections, particularly as Helen now owned the house.

"I'm going to marry an architect," Helen answered. "His name is Michael and we are very much in love."

To her surprise, her voice trembled violently as she spoke.

"I suppose he'll be pleased to hear that you own this lovely house now — if he's an architect, I mean," Diana remarked.

"Pleased? Yes, I suppose he will be."

Helen thought suddenly of Michael's annoyance when she tried to pay for her share of a meal. He was proud in so many small ways. How would he react to the idea of a wealthy wife?

Eve entered the room noisily, banging the door behind her.

"The men are burglar-proofing every-where. We never bothered before," she said pettishly.

"I prefer to keep my possessions in reasonable security," Helen said dryly.

"Your possessions!" Eve gave an angry little laugh and reached for a cigarette.

"I must go and see what they're doing. It sounds too terribly mysterious and exciting," Diana said, and fluttered through the door; they heard her calling, "Patrick! Patrick!"

"She's a fool," said Eve with flat bitterness in her tone. "She's one of the biggest fools I ever met. We're all fools, all of us, to stay here. All fools!"

She ground out her freshly lighted cigarette into the ashtray and began to pace restlessly up and down the room.

"Why are we fools?" Helen began, but Eve darted a swift look towards the door.

"Well, have you bolted and barred us all in now?" she said. "Are we safe and sound for the night?"

"If anybody manages to get inside the house or in the garage tonight, then he'll have to squeeze through a mousehole," Patrick said.

"Then we can all relax!" Eve cried, and reached out for another cigarette with trembling fingers.

"You look pale, Helen. Is your headache coming back?" Patrick asked, solicitously.

"I'm fine. A trifle tired, which is ridiculous when I've spent the whole day in bed. I don't think I'll bother to go to Stansbury tomorrow," Helen said, casually.

"You're very wise," said Roland from the doorway. "Diana is talking about getting up a picnic on the downs. You'd enjoy that, Eve."

"How charming of you to consider what I would enjoy!" Eve said.

"You're talking too much," Patrick said gently, and she bit her lip and twisted away to stare through the window.

"Excuse me a moment." Helen hurried out and up the stairs, with no clear idea as to what she intended to do, only the conviction that she could no longer bear to stay in that room of jarring voices and jangling emotion.

In her room, she snapped on the light, stood irresolute for a moment and then went over to the window. The garden below was in darkness. As Helen swished the curtains closed and turned away, the loose-hanging wallpaper met her eye.

She leaned over reluctantly, half afraid to see POOR PHOEBE printed twice with the black pencil, for the written words had about them something terrible in their pathetic intensity. The wallpaper had been ripped further than before, she realized, and pulled back the stiff paper, to see again those clumsy words, POOR PHOEBE. POOR PHOEBE, and beyond that, scrawled in the same heavy black crayon, POOR MARGARET. POOR MARGARET.

I have been wrong. Wrong, wrong, wrong! Time was too muddled before with the yesterday and the tomorrow meeting where they shouldn't meet. I was wrong about who was stupid and who was not stupid. I never could see behind faces to thoughts, never could peer behind closed lids to the eyes full of hate or love. In open eyes I never saw any love. Not for me. Not even for my sister, Sabina.

She was so pretty was Sabina. They all said she was pretty. But she could not see the evil around her until it was too late, and the child was born. Such a dear little girl, such a dear little Becky. We wanted to leave the house and go away, just the three of us — Sabina, me, and the baby. But Mr. Patrick needed the child, needed to set the mark upon her. The dancing day came closer, closer, closer. Sabina said that it would do no harm until after dancing day. I was afraid but I did what she told me to do.

And that was wrong. I should have taken little Becky and ran away. But I saw them coming over the hill, and I saw Sabina go out with Mr. Patrick and there was a ring of blood around the moon, and the rope was thin and strong. And I could not bear to wait until they came back.

I was wrong. And I am here now to stop it happening again. I must use a today mind. I know now. I know where Margaret is now. I can see the picture so clearly and there is blood again around the moon.

10

THEY did not, as it turned out, picnic on the downs the following day, nor did Helen get the opportunity of going either to the village or over to Stansbury. Heavy rain lashed the panes of the staring windows and the metallic glitter of lightning over the lowering horizon kept them prisoner at *Malcarew*.

The storm seemed to have affected them all, rendering them unfit for one another's company. Roland closeted himself in the little study, while Patrick and Diana played endless games of draughts in the library, the one with her usual liveliness muted, the other with an amused tolerant air. Eve wandered restlessly up and down the house, lighting one cigarette from the stub of another.

Helen retreated after lunch to the security of the green room and took the Bible out of the drawer, but her patient deciphering of the faded writing yielded no new information. There were, she noticed, only the three Patrick Carews mentioned in the list. Was it a coincidence that these three seemed to be sharers in the same evil, or was there something in the ancient belief that names held some intrinsic power, so that the bearer of a particular name could reach out from the shadows of the grave to influence those who bore the same appellation?

She closed the book and pushed it back into the drawer. The room was darkening and the green leaves on the wall seemed to writhe and twist, to form patterns and faces that arose from a memory not her own. Sly, mocking faces peered from between twilit foliage, watching and waiting; and struggling to overcome their malignancy was something small and frightened, reaching out to her. But when she strained her eyes and ears, it slipped away again, imperceptibly.

"I do hope it's fine on Friday," Diana mourned after dinner that evening. "It would be too dreadful if the whole thing was washed out by rain!"

"It won't rain. Patrick won't allow

it to rain on the dancing day!" Eve exclaimed.

"Do you control the elements too, Patrick?" Helen asked dryly.

"He controls everything! Didn't you know that he has unlimited powers?" Eve said, raising her glass.

Roland, his eyes on his plate, said, "We usually hold the beauty contest about three in the afternoon down in the square. The winner is crowned then, and there are the usual sideshows."

"But Helen will have to leave before that if she doesn't want to rush," Patrick said, smiling.

"Such a pity to miss it!" Diana was pouting, but she looked, thought Helen, faintly relieved.

The threatening storm swept in a wide arc over the downs but the growling of the thunder was diminished, the rain no more than a light pattering.

"It will be pretty miserable tomorrow," Patrick said. "It hardly seems worthwhile thinking of a picnic or of going over to Stansbury."

"But it'll be so dull!" Diana cried.

"Oh, you will have gaiety enough on

Friday," Patrick told her, lightly amused.

"I suppose I can wash my hair," Diana conceded. "And I do look better if I rest with a face-mask on for a few hours before a show."

"I wish the whole tiresome business was over!" Eve said pettishly. "I shall be glad when it's over! We didn't have to have it last year and now this year there are too many — "

"Time for coffee," Roland said, swiftly. "Sabina is looking forward to May Day, aren't you?"

The girl who had just entered nodded and flicked a quick, sideways smile towards Patrick.

"Shall we go into the library?" Roland said. "Helen, did you know my father had a very good coin collection? It's yours now, of course; so you might like to look at it."

He proved, she thought, quite knowledgeable on the subject, handling the bronze and silver discs with care as he related how they had been collected and mounted. Listening to his quiet, donnish voice, Helen was caught again by the notion that he seemed out of place in this family, lacking the ruthless quality that lay beneath Patrick's charm.

She excused herself shortly after tea and went upstairs. Glancing through the window as she pulled the curtains, she had the impression for a moment of a white face glimmering at her from the darkness of bush and tree. But the momentary impression faded as there was a tap on the door. Opening it, Helen was surprised to see Eve.

Roland's wife had changed into a wide sleeved housecoat of red corduroy velvet. Her face, rising out of the high, pointed collar, was startlingly white.

"What is it, Eve? Is something wrong?" Helen couldn't prevent concern even though she disliked the woman.

"On Friday when you go to fetch Kate," Eve said, in a low hurried tone, "don't return here. Don't come back here."

"Why not? Why shouldn't I come back here?" Despite herself, Helen dropped her own voice. "Why not, Eve? Margaret left this house to me."

"It's about Margaret's death. I must tell you about Margaret," Eve said, her eyes feverish. "It was — "

"Was what? *Murder?* Is that what you were going to say?" Helen caught Eve's thin wrist and said again, "Is it? Did they murder her, Eve?"

But the other had caught some sound from the landing below. Her white face flushed scarlet and she threw up her arm, wrenching free her own wrist, and ran along the upper hall to the main bedroom.

From below, Sabina said, politely, "Was there anything else you wanted?"

"Nothing, Sabina. Go to bed now, if you like."

"Thank you, miss. Good night." The clear young voice floated up the well of the stairs.

From somewhere in the house, Patrick called, "Sabina, bring a bottle of brandy up from the cellar, will you? And some of those dry biscuit things too."

Helen closed her door quietly and sat down on the bed. She knew now the reason for Eve's constant changes of mood, for her odd jerky mannerisms, her craving for liquids. The wide sleeves falling back from the upthrust arm had revealed skin spotted with puncture marks ranging in colour from bright scarlet to a brownish purple.

Roland's wife was a drug addict; to judge from the state of her arms an addict of long standing. Helen had no direct knowledge of drug addiction. It was not yet within the province of a junior schoolteacher, although some of her colleagues involved in secondary education had visited some clinics, and brought back horrifying stories of the mental and moral degeneration of the victims.

It was small wonder that Roland, loving his small daughter, preferred to keep her at school rather than expose her to the vagaries of her mother's sick nature. It must be Patrick who obtained the drugs. His frequent trips abroad could now be accounted for. Did he give them to Sabina too? A second reflection assured Helen that he did not. The girl's eyes and skin were too clear, her bearing too self-assured.

But why didn't Roland try to do something to put a stop to it? He must have loved his wife once; his eyes and voice still held a kind of weary, unwilling affection. Or was he caught up in, perhaps even profiting by, the vicious habits of his wife and brother?

Helen slept badly that night, tossing and turning, waking once to hear a soft, sighing within the room that died away as she began to sit up, forcing her mind from sleep. But the room was quiet and she fell asleep again at once.

Eve was not at the breakfast table and Patrick was buried in the morning paper. Roland, Diana volunteered, had gone over to White Meadows. It was still drizzling slightly but the clouds were lifting and Patrick, emerging briefly from the newsprint, informed them that it would be a sunny day.

"I'm going over to Stansbury," Helen said. "I suppose it'll be all right if I take the car?"

"I believe Eve intended to use it this morning," Patrick began.

"No, darling," said Diana, gaily, "Eve promised to stay home and wash and set my hair for me."

"Then I suppose it will be all right." He sounded grudging.

"I could get it checked over and filled up ready for the drive tomorrow," Helen said. "I think I'll start after lunch and take my time."

"Sabina will make up some coffee and sandwiches for you, unless you intend breaking your journey at a restaurant," he suggested.

"Coffee and a snack would be fine."

When she had finished her breakfast, she went out to the garage and drove the white car into the drive. Reversing it into the lane, she glanced up and saw Eve standing at the bedroom window. Her face was pressed against the glass, her eyes in shadow, her hands clasped tightly at her waist. She raised one hand and made a sharp, flapping motion before stepping back out of sight.

Helen frowned as she drove slowly down to the village. In the square, Lizzie Turvey was talking earnestly to another woman. As Helen slowed and stopped, the two women drifted towards her, smiling shyly.

"How is Rebecca today?" Helen enquired, winding down the window.

"Not up to much. She's failing fast

this year. We're getting ready for the big day tomorrow." Lizzie Turvey nodded towards the bunting being draped by a couple of boys within the windows of a small shop.

"I shall be very sorry to miss it," Helen said, "but I'm going off tomorrow for a day or so."

"To fetch Miss Kate? Mr. Patrick mentioned that she was coming home." Lizzie Turvey smiled, bobbed something resembling a curtsey, and moved away again.

The Bible presumably had not been missed. Patrick must have felt great anxiety when she told him she had been to visit old Rebecca, however. The old woman's erratic memory could, she reasoned, be a danger, unless it was considered too childishly unclear to be of value.

When she reached Stansbury, Helen found her way immediately to the street where Mr. Ernest's office was situated. She doubted if talking to the lawyer would produce very startling results, for he had not struck her as either astute or quick-witted, but if she explained her suspicions slowly and carefully she might at least get them straightened out in her own mind.

To her intense disappointment the door at the top of the stairs was closed. She rattled the handle and pressed the bell for several minutes before she gave up the attempt and began to descend the stairs again. She was almost at the bottom when the rattle of a bucket came from a side door, and an overalled woman with her head bound up in a turban came out into the passage.

"If it's Mr. Ernest, you're wasting your time, miss. He's away at the moment and I don't know when he'll be back," the woman said, helpfully.

"Thank you. It wasn't important."

But she was aware of a sinking in her heart. Even if the lawyer had been of no practical help, his cheerful, bouncing manner would have raised her own spirits, made her view the whole macabre situation in a more rational light.

The purpose of her visit defeated, she wandered aimlessly past the shops and turned in at a cafeteria, where she bought herself a pale cup of coffee, and sat dismally at a corner table, sipping it in what she admitted to herself was an attempt to delay her return to Linton. The cafeteria was almost empty, except for a couple of long-haired teenagers, and a woman with a child who wailed for chocolate ice-cream instead of vanilla. At the other side of the room a man was hunched over a toasted sandwich. As Helen glanced over towards him, she had the impression that he had swiftly dropped his eyes. He was, she noted, a youngish balding man with nothing familiar about him at all.

Nevertheless she was relieved when he pushed the plate away and, picking up the shabby green trilby from an empty chair, sauntered out. It was uncomfortable to be watched by a stranger, especially when one's nerves were worn ragged.

She finished her coffee, paid the bill adding an undeserved tip, and went out again into the street. As she got back into the car, she suddenly saw the man who had stared at her. He was leaning against a door-post, his head turned towards a display of nylon nightdresses, his eyes slanted towards the kerb. As Helen turned the ignition key, she remembered where she had seen him before. He had been standing in the graveyard talking to the old man with a wheelbarrow. She had driven past him on her way to the church.

Telling herself firmly that coincidences did happen and that she was a fool to allow every little incident to upset her, she let in the clutch and drove back along the Linton road. She had reached the main square when she saw Roland plodding along ahead of her.

As she drew level, he turned his head, blinked nervously and said something inaudible.

"I beg your pardon?" She pulled on the handbrake and leaned across to open the door.

"I said I didn't expect to see you back so soon. Patrick didn't realize you intended to go into Stansbury so early. He was going to offer to drive you there himself."

"Thank you, but from what I've heard of Patrick's driving, I'll trust my own inexperience!" Helen said, crisply, starting up again.

Beside her, Roland sat stiff and unrelaxed, giving an impression of both weariness and strain.

"I went to see Mr. Ernest," she said impulsively.

Roland jumped perceptibly and turned an ashen face towards her. "And did you? Did you see him?" he asked, with what appeared to be great difficulty.

"He wasn't in," she said flatly, and watched the relief shine out on his face.

She wished she could think of some question that would not betray her own suspicions, but they were turning in at the gates even as she racked her brain, Roland spoke, very quickly with his face turned away.

"Don't bring Kate back with you on Saturday. And don't come back yourself. Please, just leave quietly and don't come back."

Before she could question him, she had automatically brought the car to a stop and he wrenched open the door and was hurrying away as if some urgent errand tore him from her side.

"Did you have a good time?" That was Patrick coming to meet her with a more anxious question in his eyes.

"I hoped I might see Mr. Ernest but he was out," she said levelly.

"Ah, well, that's Paul Ernest for you! Always bouncing around. It's a marvel he sat still for long enough to pass his law exams."

Patrick opened the door and helped her out, conveying with gesture and expression that she was a frail soul who needed to be cherished.

"Diana's exclusive company does tend to become a trifle wearisome," he murmured. "You will hurry back from Cornwall, won't you?"

"Diana will be gone by then?"

"Oh yes," said Patrick with a coolness that appalled her. "Yes, by the time you return, I think I can guarantee that Diana won't be here."

A voice hailed them from across the garden. Roland, having apparently made a tour of the house, was standing at the front door, with a look of deep concern on his face.

"Eve? Have you seen Eve anywhere? She's not in her room and some of her clothes have gone."

"Nonsense!" Patrick dropped Helen's arm and went over to his brother.

"It's not nonsense! She isn't there, I tell you."

"You haven't looked properly," Patrick said, firmly.

"I didn't look under the bed or behind the wardrobe, if that's what you mean," Roland said, weakly sarcastic.

"Then how do you know her clothes are missing?" Helen demanded.

"The wardrobe door was open and there were several gaps on the racks," Roland told them.

"Where's Diana?" Helen asked.

"I'm right here. Is something wrong? I heard you calling for Eve." Diana fluttered out to stand by Roland.

"Eve seems to be missing," Patrick said.

"Missing? But she was in her room. She hadn't been down yet this morning."

"Then she's sulking somewhere. You know she's liable to do that," Patrick said, reasonably.

"We'd better all take a look." Helen pushed past them and went up the stairs, calling as she went.

The big lilac and silver room was in a state of extreme untidiness, the sheets and blankets ruffled, the jars and bottles on the dressing table without their lids, towels crumpled on the carpet. Eve's heady perfume hung heavily in the close atmosphere. The wardrobe door was open and there were several empty hangers among the close packed rows of dresses and suits.

"Can you tell what exactly is missing?" Helen asked Roland who had just entered the room.

"Eve had so many clothes," Roland said vaguely. "She was always buying new things. Her tweed trouser-suit isn't there. She bought it last month and then decided she didn't like the colour. Her mink jacket has gone too, and a blue dress she had with gold beading on the hem. That's funny!"

"What's funny?" Diana demanded.

"She hung up a couple of bathing suits that she didn't wear any longer, to remind herself to give them to Sabina. Eve hasn't been swimming for several years," he said, awkwardly.

"The suits are both gone. And an old

green coat that was out of style. It isn't here."

"Her handbag? Is that gone too?" Diana asked.

"She had several." Roland looked around in the same vague fashion. "Her current favourite was a black suede one. Big and square. She said it held most of her junk."

"Isn't it here?"

"She kept it on the armchair. It doesn't seem to be here now."

"Where did she keep her jewellery?" Helen asked.

"In a blue velvet box on the dressing table. It's not there."

"There's no sign of Eve anywhere in the house or garden," Patrick said from the landing. "Are any of her clothes missing?"

"Quite a selection," Helen told him.

"Have any suitcases been taken?" Patrick asked.

"She had matching luggage," Roland said, "dark green, with her initials on them. They were stored over in the wall cupboard."

"Is this it?" Diana pointed to another

partly open door. "Is one of the suitcases missing?"

"I think so. There should be six but there only seem to be five." Roland blinked at them helplessly.

"Then it looks as if darling Eve has taken a little trip," Patrick observed. "I warned you she was liable to break out one day."

"But didn't either of you hear her leave?" Helen asked.

"We've been in the library all morning, discussing wedding plans. We had the door closed," Diana said, looking coy.

"Did Sabina or the other girl see her go?"

"They've been in the kitchen the whole time as far as I know," Patrick said.

"But she wouldn't leave without telling me," Roland protested.

"She's threatened to do so," Patrick said.

"All women threaten to leave their husbands. Most of them never do," Roland said.

"Eve isn't most women. You ought not to need me to tell you that," Patrick said with quiet and deadly contempt.

"Where would she go? She must have taken the car. The sports car is still in the garage, isn't it?"

"Then she caught the bus," Diana suggested.

"Did she have any money with her?" Helen asked.

"She usually kept about forty pounds in her purse and she had a cheque book," said Roland.

"Then she's taken off! I wouldn't worry about it if I were you," Patrick said briskly. "She'll probably come crawling back. You know how she loves to be the centre of attention."

"Wouldn't it be a good idea to inform the police? She may be ill," Helen suggested, thinking of the bright eyes and twitching hands, the hoarse voice warning her not to return.

"Inform them of what?" Patrick shrugged. "A grown woman has a perfect right to pack a suitcase and walk out on her husband."

"I suppose so," Roland muttered.

"I think we ought to carry on as if nothing had happened," Diana said. "Why should Eve be allowed to spoil things? I call it very selfish of her. And she'd promised to do my hair this afternoon too! Helen, are you good at setting hair? Would you help me with mine?"

Helen nodded absently, her eyes straying around the untidy room, so like Eve's nature in its excessive luxury and lack of purpose.

So Eve, she thought, was frightened, so frightened that she had packed a suitcase and fled. She had taken her handbag and her jewellery, her mink jacket and blue dress — and a suit she didn't like, an unfashionable coat, and two discarded bathing suits? Would Eve, elegant despite her deterioration, snatch up clothes that she had no intention of wearing, or had somebody else hurriedly removed a pile of garments to give the impression of flight?

11

AFTER lunch Helen washed and set Diana's hair and then submitted to having her own hair pinned up into a variety of exotic styles.

"You'd have made a lovely show-girl, you really would!" Diana exclaimed, bestowing what she evidently considered to be the highest praise. "If you took off five or six pounds weight and wore spike heels and feathers, you'd get into a really top-line club."

Helen had a momentary vision of herself entering the school staffroom in feathers and high heels and choked back a giggle. There was something blessedly normal about Diana, something that pushed the shadows back into the corners where they belonged.

At dinner time, it was Diana who chattered while Roland and Helen made spasmodic attempts to respond. Patrick said nothing, but leaned back and let his bright sardonic gaze rove round the table. In contrast to Roland who re-filled his wine glass several times, Patrick drank sparingly.

The evening dragged. Roland got up frequently and went over to the window, staring out as if he expected to see Eve coming across the lawn. Yet her name was not mentioned, just as Margaret's name was never spoken unless Helen herself brought it up.

Long after she had gone to bed, Helen lay wakeful, staring into the darkness. There would, she considered, be the whole of the following day before she need become active on Diana's behalf. No doubt the village fête would pass off innocently enough, but after darkness had fallen there would be a gathering at *Malcarew*; and another young girl would disappear like the one called Carla who had vanished two years before, and Rebecca Linton's mother who had vanished when the old woman was a baby. That had been about the same time as the servant girl had hanged herself.

"Did you try to escape that way, Phoebe?" Helen whispered into the darkness, and heard no whisper in reply; but the sense of being watched with aching sympathy was so strong that she felt a quick turn of her head would bring her companion into view.

Eve was dead! Helen knew that as clearly as if she had seen it with eyes other than her own. Either Eve had proved a danger to be removed, or she had been driven to suicide, and the facts suppressed, the evidence twisted, to make it look as if she had left. But Diana and Patrick had been together all morning, so it must have been done the previous night. Roland slept in the same room, so what value could be placed on his fussing and fretting? It could so easily be an act put on to impress Diana and herself.

Helen fell asleep, thinking of Diana, who flitted through a vague dream later on, wearing a green trilby hat and Sabina's blue overall.

Friday was a sunny day. Helen's first thought when she awoke was the uncomplicated realization that the village fête wouldn't be spoiled; but immediately upon that thought followed the chilling recognition that the fête was only the outward, civilized disguise for an older ceremony.

In the library after breakfast, she took down the heavy Local Encyclopaedia and read steadily, each word giving substance to her fears. The first day of May in pre-Christian times had been Walpurgis Day, a great Sabbat of the devotees of the Horned god. It was the time when, in small, rural communities all over England, wives crept from their husband's beds, and daubing themselves with the hallucogenic ointment which made them believe themselves capable of flying, hurried with their lighted torches up the hill towards the ancient place of sacrifice.

Helen closed the book, put it back and turned, with forced amiability, as Diana came in with some dresses over her arm and the earnest request that Helen help her to choose one to wear at the contest.

"The green one is rather super, but Patrick likes me in white. The men have gone down to the village to find out if Eve caught the bus yesterday. I don't blame her if she did leave, do you? It's dull here even with Patrick, but if one were married to Roland!" Diana gave an exaggerated shudder and laughed.

Helen opened her mouth with the vague intention of sounding a warning, any warning that might alert the girl to the dangers of the coming night. But she left the sentence unspoken. Diana would either refuse to believe her or else panic and reveal her fear to Patrick and Roland. There was no certainty then that either of them would get away. As it was, Helen was free to leave, free to fetch Kate. She dare not risk losing that chance of freedom.

"If I were you, I'd wear the one that Patrick likes," she said, aloud.

When they met for lunch, Patrick presented her with a map of the route to Kate's school and a brief letter of introduction to the headmistress.

"Sabina has made sandwiches and coffee for the journey," he told her. "There's a pretty spot just off the main road — here." He indicated the place on the map.

"Has there been any news of Eve?" Diana asked.

"Not as far as we know, but she may have got on the bus without being particularly noticed. A number of people went over to Stansbury yesterday; most of them women getting their hair done. I tell you, she'll be back within a few days, probably sooner if she discovers we haven't abandoned the festivities to go chasing after her," Patrick said, with a smiling nod towards his brother who was again eating scarcely anything and drinking a great deal.

It was past two o'clock when they rose from the table, and Patrick helped Helen solicitously into the car, handing in her overnight case and the square wicker picnic basket. Despite the pleasant tones of his voice, the warmth of his hand as it rested briefly on her own, she was conscious of his intense desire to see her leave.

"The contest is at three. Wish me luck!" Diana trilled from the doorway.

Helen smiled and waved, evaded the meaning look in Patrick's eyes, and drove slowly away from the widely shining windows.

She would have to drive for an hour

for fear somebody decided to follow her. In any case there was no doing anything until they were all out of the house and down in the village. Although she looked back once or twice, the road behind was clear, and after a while, with the streamer-decked village behind, she found she could relax a little, driving slowly while she worked out the final details of her plan.

It was delightfully warm and at any other time she would have enjoyed herself, but there was so much to be done. She hoped she would prove equal to the task she had set herself, but even here, on an empty road, tentacles of evil seemed to reach out towards her.

She drew up into a side road and reached into the back of the car for the picnic basket. The sandwiches looked tempting, and, when she unscrewed the top of the vacuum flask, the aroma of freshly ground coffee rose up into the clear air.

Helen opened the car door and swung her legs over the side. She would allow herself ten minutes and then turn back and circle round to Stansbury. A rustle from the bank caused her to jump violently, and a jet of hot coffee spurted out across the grass. She drew her legs back sharply and looked down at the tip of her shoe where a few drops of the liquid had splashed. The leather of the shoe had blistered and shredded, and in sudden horrified revulsion, she threw the flask away from her, saw it describe an arc and fall again, its contents burning and blackening the grass.

"And I almost drank it," she said aloud, and felt as limp and weak as a rag doll.

Sabina! Sabina had made the sandwiches and the coffee. Sabina was young, ill-educated; the niceties of legal procedure would mean nothing to her. No doubt Patrick had not even bothered to explain everything to her. But Sabina had feared Helen's return, and had decided to get rid of the usurper, without thinking beyond the immediate consequences of her action.

Slamming the door, Helen gripped the wheel and backed out into the main road again. She forced herself to drive carefully, resisting the temptation to press her foot down hard on the accelerator.

It took longer than she expected to work out a road that would by-pass Linton and bring her directly into Stansbury. It was past five when she pulled into the main shopping centre, where a few late shoppers were buying groceries before the Saturday morning rush.

"Miss Clifton! Miss Clifton!"

As the noise of the engine died, the voice rang out, it seemed above all the surrounding noises.

"Mr. Ernest!" Helen was shaking with relief. He bounced to the side of the car and looked at her with alarm all over his chubby face.

"My dear Miss Clifton, you look quite ill. What has happened? Have you already been told?"

"Told what?" She stared at him.

"Mrs. Carew. Mrs. Eve Carew is dead. Apparently it was murder." He brought out the word doubtfully as if it were a stone of dubious value.

"I know. I guessed. Margaret too," she said dully, and he leaned across and patted her shoulder in a bewildered fashion.

The police have gone to *Malcarew*. I'm supposed to wait until the local magistrate arrives. To swear out a warrant, I think. You'd better go straight back. As far as I know there's a patrol car out looking for you."

"Acid," she said breathlessly. "There was acid in the coffee. Sabina made a mistake, you see."

"You'll have to give evidence," he told her.

"Evidence, yes." That was what she had intended to go back to find while the Carews were down in the village.

"I'm not very brave," she said to Mr. Ernest. "I hoped that it wouldn't be necessary to go back and search. I wouldn't have known really where to look."

"Will you let me get you some coffee? It would make you feel better," he suggested.

But she shook her head. "It'll be a long time before I can face a cup of coffee again," she said, tremulously.

"Then I'll go back to the station and

228

tell them to pull in their patrol cars. I'll
follow you as soon as Langley arrives."

She drew a deep breath and started
the car.

"How was — how do they know it was
murder?" she turned to ask. "Where was
she — found?"

"Don't know any more than you do
yet. Nobody tells lawyers anything," he
said, sulky and petulant as a small boy
deprived of a treat. "I just hope I don't
miss any of the investigations. The chance
might not come again."

"You might be lucky!" she exclaimed
in sarcasm, and drove away past the
late shoppers into the blue haze of the
climbing road.

As she approached Linton her foot
eased on the accelerator. The thought
of passing through the village was
unpleasant as if it lay between her and
safety, but her arrival was unnoticed.
People were moving about the square
laden with paper-hats and candy floss and
cheap trinkets they had acquired from the
stalls erected around. Coloured streamers
trailed dismally across cobblestones littered
with toffee wrappers and cigarette ends.

In the centre a maypole stood, its coloured ribbons fluttering.

Helen edged the car between chattering teenagers and began to drive up the hill. A warrant to be sworn out, Mr. Ernest had said. Somebody had been detained already then.

The front door stood open, a sign that the police were within. Perhaps Mr. Ernest had meant a search warrant. The police would need it, she supposed.

Within the hall the doors were closed. Helen opened the one leading into the sitting-room but the apartment was empty. Presumably officialdom preferred the splendours of the gold and white drawing-room. But that apartment was also empty. So was the library and when she opened the door leading to the kitchen quarters and called, only the echo of her own voice answered her.

The police should have arrived. They should be taking fingerprints and making notes and getting on good terms with the kitchen staff. Nice, comfortable, deep-voiced men doing all the things she had read about in books.

She went up the stairs, treading

carefully as if someone were asleep in the house. On the lower landing she paused, listening, but there was no sign or sound. The doors leading from the upper landing were flung open, the rooms within left tidy or untidy as they had been when she left. As she reached the door of her own room, the front door slammed shut.

She turned, waiting for the heavy footsteps, the brisk voices; but there was only the silence of the house, pressing around her, so that to speak herself, even to move quickly, became a physical impossibility.

There had been, she remembered, no police cars at the gate, no guards at the door. They had not after all arrived yet.

"The wind made the door bang," she whispered aloud, and tried to change the image in her mind from a heavy, oaken door to a light one of plywood that would move in the slightest breeze.

The wallpaper had been ripped almost entirely from the wall and the crayon marks stood out, black and straggling.

POOR PHOEBE. POOR PHOEBE.

POOR MARGARET. POOR MARGARET.

POOR HELEN. POOR HELEN.

And poor Eve and poor Tom Weaver, she thought. Their names have been left out. And there is no need for me to stay here alone. I can drive back to the village and wait there.

She would have to pull back her door first. But it had been open when she entered the room. She had noticed that all the doors were open on this floor.

All she had to do was go over to the door and pull it back, turn left and descend the shallow steps, walk across the landing, turn right and go down the main staircase, cross the hall and lift the latch on the heavy oaken door. Then she would be out in the sunshine, near to the car. Even if the car had gone or wouldn't start, she could still run, couldn't she? Down the lane, past the cottages, into the square with its fluttering maypole ribbons.

There was a faint, sighing sound from beyond the door as if someone had drawn an exasperated breath. She felt the hairs at the back of her neck quiver as if a cold wind had entered the room.

Somebody tapped gently on the door. It was not a clear-cut knock, more a hesitant sliding of knuckles across the wood.

Helen moistened her lips, forced them to shape the words.

"Come in," she said, and was astonished when the two words sounded out loud.

The door moved inward slowly and a figure stood upon the threshold. The newcomer wore a neat grey suit and had hair curling over her head. Her shoes were low-heeled, a mink jacket hung with casual elegance from her shoulders and red lips smiled, widely, mockingly, as Helen moved back, pressing herself between bed and window, as if trying desperately to escape.

"Dear, *dear* Helen! You can't think how eagerly I've waited for this moment," the figure drawled.

And slamming the door behind her, Margaret walked into the room.

12

"**Y**OU haven't changed at all," Margaret said. "How strange that you should remain exactly as I always picture you! A little pale, perhaps? But that's understandable, isn't it? You did think I was dead."

"Murdered. I thought you had been murdered." Helen's voice was a whisper.

"What a quaint idea! Did you ever really think that I was the type of young woman who gets murdered?"

"No," Helen said slowly. "No."

Margaret had not changed either. Yet, looking at her, Helen felt as if she had never seen the other before. Surely Margaret's eyes had never been so hard when they had talked together over coffee late at night in the hostel.

"But then you never really thought about me at all, did you, Helen?" Margaret said. "I was the plain-faced friend, who could be relied upon to listen sympathetically when your current

234

boy-friend didn't turn up, or you were worried because your lipstick didn't match your new dress."

"You were my friend," Helen said.

"I was never anybody's friend," Margaret said harshly. "Other people made use of me, that's all! I was 'good old Margaret' who stitched up hems, and cut thick slices of chocolate cake when you came in from your dates, and passed the examinations without any bother because, never having any dates myself, I had plenty of time to study."

"But I *was* your friend!"

"You threw me an occasional letter telling me how happy you were in your snug little flat, with your snug little job and your snug little love affair. Dear Helen always pitied the misfits and tried to help them."

"But you married a rich man. That was what you wanted, wasn't it?"

"Oh, indeed I did. Next to love, power is important. And money can buy power. Shall I tell you how I came to marry Donald Carew?"

"Yes. Yes, tell me."

If she could keep her talking, anybody

might come. The police. Mr. Ernest. Anybody!

"I went to Italy on holiday, a treat for a spinster schoolteacher! I met Patrick there. I don't know even now why he stopped to talk to me, but it was as if we recognized one another. Anyway, we went about together. He told me about himself, about his family living in the same small village for generations, wielding power over a little corner of the earth."

Her flat, expressionless voice was more terrifying than any excitement could have been.

"He told me," she continued, "that once one of his ancestors with the same Christian name as himself had sold his soul to the devil, practised the dark arts, and been hanged at the last because he killed a village girl during the sacrificial rite. And his own great-grandfather had the same name and nature. Patrick Carew had built a fine new house — this house — and lived in it and every year at the May Festival, on the dancing day, chose a girl from the village to play her part when the fires were lit."

"The girl died?"

"No, why should she die? It was her privilege to mate with the leader of the revels, with the devil-deputy. But there were accidents. The girl might protest or threaten to inform, and then she would have to be silenced."

"Sabina was silenced," Helen said, without knowing what she intended to say. "Sabina Linton bore Patrick Carew a child, a girl named Rebecca. But Sabina was afraid and wanted to leave. Only Patrick persuaded her to stay for one more dancing day but it was her last. He killed her so that he could keep the child, put the witchmark on the child. And the housemaid hanged herself because she hadn't the courage to try to stop it. That frightened Patrick so he gave up the dancing days and hushed the scandal. But the people in the village guessed about Rebecca, and no man would marry her. She was close on forty before she found a husband and they had only the one girl."

"What has all this to do with my story?" Margaret frowned. "Patrick had an old nurse called Rebecca. She told him bits of things about his ancestors. He found out the rest from the records in the old church. He burned them when he'd read them — almost burned down the church at the same time!"

A crow of laughter escaped her.

"Patrick wanted to revive the old ways? Was that it?" Helen asked.

"He was bored," said Margaret. "He was only the younger brother but he was stronger, more intelligent, more attractive than Roland ever was. Their father despised them both, the one for his weakness, the other because his birth killed his mother."

"But Roland married and had a child!"

"Eve was a nobody," Margaret said. "A nobody who was Patrick's mistress for a while until he brought her here and pushed her on to Roland."

"And supplied her with drugs so that she would continue to do what he wanted her to do," Helen said slowly.

"But it wasn't enough," Margaret said. "It wasn't enough. He wanted to revive the old ways, and some of the villagers knew something of those ways. Knew them and might be persuaded to follow them. The Carews still owned the land, and these country folk are still superstitious."

"Carla! Who was Carla?" Helen demanded.

"A silly little virgin whom Patrick had taken home," Margaret said. "He told her they were going to be married of course, but at the last moment when she learned about the dancing day, she ran away. And the old man, Patrick's father, found out what had been planned and threatened to leave his property to charity and not to his own two sons."

"And Patrick told you all this!"

"We were drawn together," said Margaret. "We were the same people — the same aims and ambitions. We were the same."

"Evil to evil," Helen said bitterly, and Margaret smiled with joy lightening her heavy face.

"Evil. Pure evil," she said. "There is nothing that brings one so much power!"

"And so you married old Mr. Carew."

"He didn't know I'd met Patrick, of course. He thought of me as the temporary governess he'd engaged for his little grand-daughter, Kate. He was a feeble old man, disappointed in his family, eager for friendship. And I was always such a good helpful friend." Margaret's voice was harsh. "I married him and I was such a good, docile wife. And he died quite naturally in the end, leaving me all his fortune, except for the allowances for his sons and the trust-fund for Kate."

"And he left you *Malcarew*."

"Whoever owns *Malcarew* owns Linton," Margaret said. "Between us, Patrick and I could bring back the old days, recreate the past. We planned so carefully and Patrick found a girl for the dancing day. He wrote and told me about his new 'fiancée'. I laughed to think of it."

"But why me? Why did you bring me here?"

"To kill you, of course, in the end." Margaret's voice was as calm as if she were discussing the weather. "I knew you'd come if I asked for help. So I wrote that pathetic little note, and it brought you."

"But I saw your grave!"

"Anybody can replace one wooden cross by another," Margaret said serenely. "There was a danger, of course, that you might demand to see a death certificate but you never did, and there was the chance you might start gossiping to the wrong people in the village, but you never did that either. Anyway there is no satisfaction in doing something when there is no risk in it."

"But why do it at all? Why not kill me and be done with it?"

"But I was dead," Margaret said, "and you had inherited my property. Didn't it give you a feeling of power, to imagine for a little while that you were rich?"

"You put the acid in the coffee flask."

"Patrick followed you with Paul Ernest," the other explained. "If you had done as you were told and stopped to drink the coffee, Ernest would have simply turned your car around and driven it back to *Malcarew*, leaving a suicide by the verge of the road. By the time you were found and identified, there would have been nothing to connect you with Linton. Patrick will go to your flat as soon as the ceremony is finished and destroy anything there that connects you with us."

"I wrote to Michael, and to my school," Helen said, "telling them what had happened. I posted the letters myself."

"And the postman is Lizzie Turvey's brother."

"I told people that I was coming here."

"We will all say that you never arrived."

"Paul Ernest isn't Paul Ernest?"

"Oh, yes, indeed. His father, the family lawyer, is on holiday at the moment. Paul himself was disbarred a year ago."

"Tom Weaver? You killed him, didn't you?"

"When old Turvey died, Weaver applied for the job. I didn't want strangers around the place, but Roland was stupid enough to engage him. He was away the weekend I 'died'. But he poked and pried around, went up into Eve's room and found heroin, tried to warn Sabina. Sabina, of all people!"

"You put the dummy in the car."

"Sometimes we use dummies at the

ceremony. It seemed like a good joke. I didn't even tell Patrick what I was going to do."

"And you killed Eve? Because she was going to talk to me?"

"She was losing her nerve," said Margaret. "Drug addicts lose all sense of reality after a time, become incapable of logical reasoning. I killed her and took some of her clothes, to make Roland think that she had run away. He still had an unfortunate weakness for his wife. He didn't know about Weaver either. Patrick's brother doesn't have the stomach for murder. He thought that we were all playing a particularly nasty practical joke on you."

"But he gave Sabina a hundred pounds."

"Why shouldn't he give his daughter a little present?" Margaret enquired.

"Daughter?"

"The one positive action poor Roland ever took was to get Rebecca's daughter with child. Can you imagine it? A stammering boy of nineteen and a county bumpkin past thirty! It was hushed up at the time and Mary Linton bundled off to the States. Even old Rebecca wasn't told the full story, but the rest of us knew. Except for little Kate, of course. One day, when she is old enough to understand or when Roland begins to assert himself too much, then loving Uncle Patrick may introduce her to her half-sister."

"You said Phoebe was your only friend — "

"Oh, the name on the wall? The wallpaper came loose one day and I noticed the writing. Some child must have scribbled it at some time or other. I put it in the letter, to provide you with a little extra mystery. You always used to enjoy crossword puzzles. As far as I know," Margaret sauntered to the door, "Phoebe doesn't exist."

"But she *does* exist," Helen said aloud, as the door closed. "I know she exists. She knows what to do to stop this thing. She knows the words and the gestures that will end the evil. And she has to help me now."

She sat in the darkening room, her chin in her hands, trying to force back the waves of fear coursing through her limbs, trying to empty her mind even of schemes for escape. There were no sounds but the ticking of the clock and her own deliberately even breathing. She had lost count of time, could feel the shackling of her limbs, heavy limbs, earth limbs. There was a whispering in her head; a whispering in the room; a stirring among the twisting leaves on the green wall.

Her eyelids drooped and then rose again, her eyes fixing themselves on the shape that could not be seen, in the shadow where the shadow was darkest. It was colder now, a creeping shivering cold with a whimpering at the core of it like the whimpering of a child. But it was a child, who moved with a girl's body and unformed mind to the coil of rope on the floor, and stood, !ooping the rope between work roughened hands.

"Not this time, Phoebe! Not this time."

The unspoken words set up a quivering in the shadows as if two worlds met and merged, and Helen's mind stretched wider, empty, awaiting its guest.

"Sitting here all by yourself in the dark?" Margaret asked, genially. "But it's

245

time now for the ceremony to begin."

The girl within the room rose docilely and followed through the door and down the stairs. In the hall, Margaret indicated the kitchen quarters.

"We'll go through this way and cut through the vegetable garden to the downs," she said, briskly. "Please don't try anything stupid. An undignified tussle wouldn't help either of us. Now what is it?"

"Water? I need a glass of water."

"Well, take one then," Margaret said, and nodded impatiently to the shelves where the tumblers were ranged above kitchen condiments and egg-cups.

A tumbler crashed down between the other's trembling hands, causing Margaret to jump back sharply.

"Leave it!" she exclaimed. "We'll be late."

The other, hands deep in the pockets where she had thrust the cellar of salt and the little bottle of olive oil, nodded and went ahead through the door into the sloping garden. Once, as the pungent scent of rosemary rose up in the gloom, she stumbled to one knee and was yanked up, her fingers clutching tufts of the grey-green foliage.

It was as she had remembered it, with the white stone glimmering in the darkness and the circle of robed figures bearing their torches. Yet it was not quite the same for the circle was much smaller than it should have been. Lizzie Turvey was there, and a younger woman, holding between them old Rebecca who nodded and muttered in bewildered fashion. Paul Ernest looked like Friar Tuck in his bunched robe, and Gladys had her mouth open as if she were about to scream with hysteria. There were two or three hooded figures there but she could identify none of them.

"They've begun!" Margaret hissed in savage disappointment, as she thrust a way into the circle. "They began without us!"

Patrick stepped forward out of the blackness beyond the stone. He looked taller than by day, the cloak of red and silver symbols falling back like wings as he raised the communion cup in his hands, and arching his head on which a horned skullcap glinted, said very deep and sure, "In the name of Lucifer, Prince of Darkness. Drink. In the name of Lucifer, Lord of the World. Drink."

Sabina was coming forward, her eyes glowing, leading the slim figure in white draperies with a wreath of May blossom on her head. Diana walked slowly, her arms down by her sides, her eyes half-closed.

The cup, with its abominable contents, was being passed from hand to hand, mouths opening like black caverns to drink. There should be a cock or a goat on the flat stone, to provide liquid for the second passing of the cup, but there was only Diana standing with her arms by her sides and the wreath on her fair hair.

"Drink!" said Margaret, and handed the heavy vessel to her companion.

The ceremony excites her so much, the girl thought, that she has forgotten for a moment I am to be killed.

Slowly, she took the cup and tilted it upside-down towards the grass. There was a second's pause as if the forces of evil withdrew for an instant in order to regroup and then stream forth with renewed vigour. They were caught in that second like figures on a frieze; and then she rushed forward, throwing salt and oil and tufts of rosemary at the circle of hooded figures while words spilled out of her.

"Begone in the name of the Father. Azael, Mechitophel, Beelzebub, Achitophel, Lucifer. Begone."

The figure in the symbolled cloak raised his arm and flung the curved knife hidden in his sleeve. She lurched side ways and fell, hearing Margaret's high, animal screech as she stood with the hilt of the knife protruding from her ribs, and then the sickening crunching sound as she fell forwards.

All hell broke loose in swinish grunts and groans and yells, as concentrated evil was broken into fragments and the silent circle became a mass of writhing, screaming people.

But I was in my room, Helen thought. How did I get here? And how am I going to get Diana away?

She took an uncertain step forward but a tall man had seized her and pinioned her arms and was pulling her out of the patch of trampled grass.

Patrick was running towards them, and his face in the glaring light was twisted as a satyr's. She squirmed in the tall man's grasp, biting the hand that held her captive, and kicking at his shins. And then Patrick, hands outstretched, stopped dead as if he were listening to the report that had rung out, and crumpled at her feet. Over his body she looked towards Diana and saw the girl, the sleep-walking look vanished, with a pistol in her hand.

Men were running towards them and the darkness was stabbed by a dozen torches. The man holding Helen pushed her roughly to one side, and strode over to Lizzie Turvey who was rocking to and fro and screaming obscenities. Paul Ernest had gathered up his robes and was running awkwardly into the arms of a uniformed figure.

She staggered back to the low white wall, watching the crazily swirling scene as if it were some pageant staged for her benefit. The tall man was by her side, swabbing blood from his wrist with the corner of his robe and grinning ruefully.

"You have a sound set of teeth, Miss Clifton! It was impossible for me to get at my gun," he remarked.

"I didn't recognize you," Helen gasped, "without your green trilby hat!"

"Detective Inspector John Welby, Miss Clifton. I'm sorry you ever noticed me at all, but Diana and I couldn't be sure, in the beginning, if you were part of the whole unpleasant set-up or not."

"Diana?"

"Diana Harris is a very efficient undercover agent with the Narcotics Bureau. She and I have worked together on several cases, involving the illegal sale of drugs. You'd better come back to the house. The Stansbury police will round up the rest of them."

Legs weak, she clung to his arm as they descended the slope and re-entered the house. There were lights in every room and policemen were standing in the hall.

"Three cups of tea, if you please." The inspector was as urbane as if they had just walked into a restaurant.

"We'd had our eye on Mr. Patrick

Carew for some time," the tall man said conversationally, ushering her into the library. "But he was a slippery fish; too clever to work with the same people all the time. Then young Carla Reynolds came with some greatly delayed information she'd just plucked up the courage to impart, and we got on his track again. We provided him with a new fiancée, very pretty and rather dim, and Diana can act exceedingly dimly when she chooses."

"If only she'd told me!"

"How could she? You turned up out of the blue, and by the time we'd checked that Margaret Carew wasn't dead and that you were exactly what you claimed to be, by then Diana judged it better for you to get out of the way and set off to collect the child. She didn't know Margaret intended to kill you."

"With acid!" Helen said, and shuddered.

"Nasty habits these people acquire!" the inspector said sadly. "Ah, here's Diana, and the tea. Both very welcome!"

"I can really do with this," Diana said, cheerfully. "I had to pretend to drink the drugged stuff they gave me."

She still wore the filmy white dress and flower-wreath, but her voice was sharper, her bearing assured.

"Roland Carew? I haven't seen him," Helen remembered.

"Apparently he usually gets very drunk on these occasions, but this time they went too far when he suspected they killed his wife. He gave himself up this afternoon. Fortunately he had the good sense to play his part by returning to the house and downing a bottle of whisky. His sentence should be a light one. We found Eve Carew and Tom Weaver, by the way."

"Eve was in the car-pit; Weaver in the cellar of Becky Linton's house," said Diana. "She'd been strangled."

"Probably after I left the house, while you and Patrick were in the library. Margaret?"

"She was sleeping down in the cellar, but I didn't realize that until it was too late. I blame myself for Eve's death, but it hadn't occurred to me that she was in any danger."

"And Weaver?"

"Had been stabbed. Margaret Carew

apparently tried to vary her methods of murder. Weaver got curious about Eve's drug-taking and unwisely took Sabina into his confidence. And I think he must have had half-formed suspicions about Margaret's sudden 'death' and your timely arrival."

"Paul Ernest and Sabina Linton will be indicted for murder," the inspector said. "The other maid too, though she's so retarded I doubt if any jury will convict. The others, Lizzie Turvey and those from the village who were present tonight will certainly stand trial for fraud though it's doubtful if evidence of a more serious kind will be found against them. The old woman will be cared for; she's too old to realize what was involved."

"But *you* seemed to know!" Diana exclaimed. "What was all that business with the salt-cellar and the twigs? And that invocation you chanted? What was all that about?"

"I don't know," Helen began.

"Oil and salt were among the elements used to cleanse a house of evil spirits, weren't they?" the inspector remarked. "And I think rosemary used to be nailed over doors at one time to keep witches away."

"Then I must have read it somewhere," Helen said, uncertainly.

"The whole thing was too weird!" Diana exclaimed. "Fancy trying to revive Satanic sacrifices in the second part of the twentieth century! But he looked effective in that strange cloak, didn't he? I felt quite ineffectual for a moment, even though I had the gun in my pocket and knew the inspector had insinuated himself into the circle. If one believed in evil — !"

She shrugged and laughed.

"Don't you?" Helen asked, curiously.

"In evil people, yes. Drug-trafficking is a particularly vicious trade. But in pure evil, dark powers, all that mumbo jumbo, *no!*"

"This is a nice bit of property," the inspector said, glancing round the room. "It will be young Kate Carew's now, I daresay. Or her father's, to be more precise, though he won't be occupying it for a year or two."

"Lovely indeed, but too big for my liking!" Diana exclaimed.

"Kate will be happy here," Helen said.

"And she's a nice child from all accounts, despite her relations," the inspector nodded.

"I'll be returning to my own flat in the morning," Helen said. "You'll want me to give evidence, I suppose."

"When we've sorted it all out," Diana said. "Mounds of paperwork and statements and bits of evidence. I hate the donkeywork."

"There'll be police in and out all night, I'm afraid." The tall man sounded apologetic. "Can you manage to snatch a few hours' sleep? We'll concentrate on the murders and the narcotics angle. The other business is so far-fetched that we're liable to weaken our case if we lay too much emphasis on that aspect."

So that is how it ends, Helen thought, as she climbed the stairs. Tomorrow I go back to the job I thought I had left, to the man I want to marry. And Kate will inherit this house and grow up to be stronger than her father.

She went into the small green room and stood for a moment before switching on the light, thinking of a restless soul returning to avert an evil once avoided by the wrong means.

She said out loud, in a tremulous questioning tone, "Phoebe? Phoebe?"

But in the darkness, nothing stirred.

THE END

THE WILDERNESS WALK
Sheila Bishop

Stifling unpleasant memories of a misbegotten romance in Cleave with Lord Francis Aubrey, Lavinia goes on holiday there with her sister. The two women are thrust into a romantic intrigue involving none other than Lord Francis.

THE RELUCTANT GUEST
Rosalind Brett

Ann Calvert went to spend a month on a South African farm with Theo Borland and his sister. They both proved to be different from her first idea of them, and there was Storr Peterson — the most disturbing man she had ever met.

ONE ENCHANTED SUMMER
Anne Tedlock Brooks

A tale of mystery and romance and a girl who found both during one enchanted summer.

CLOUD OVER MALVERTON
Nancy Buckingham

Dulcie soon realises that something is seriously wrong at Malverton, and when violence strikes she is horrified to find herself under suspicion of murder.

AFTER THOUGHTS
Max Bygraves

The Cockney entertainer tells stories of his East End childhood, of his RAF days, and his post-war showbusiness successes and friendships with fellow comedians.

MOONLIGHT
AND MARCH ROSES
D. Y. Cameron

Lynn's search to trace a missing girl takes her to Spain, where she meets Clive Hendon. While untangling the situation, she untangles her emotions and decides on her own future.

NURSE ALICE IN LOVE
Theresa Charles

Accepting the post of nurse to little Fernie Sherrod, Alice Everton could not guess at the romance, suspense and danger which lay ahead at the Sherrod's isolated estate.

POIROT INVESTIGATES
Agatha Christie

Two things bind these eleven stories together — the brilliance and uncanny skill of the diminutive Belgian detective, and the stupidity of his Watson-like partner, Captain Hastings.

LET LOOSE THE TIGERS
Josephine Cox

Queenie promised to find the long-lost son of the frail, elderly murderess, Hannah Jason. But her enquiries threatened to unlock the cage where crucial secrets had long been held captive.

THE TWILIGHT MAN
Frank Gruber

Jim Rand lives alone in the California desert awaiting death. Into his hermit existence comes a teenage girl who blows both his past and his brief future wide open.

DOG IN THE DARK
Gerald Hammond

Jim Cunningham breeds and trains gun dogs, and his antagonism towards the devotees of show spaniels earns him many enemies. So when one of them is found murdered, the police are on his doorstep within hours.

THE RED KNIGHT
Geoffrey Moxon

When he finds himself a pawn on the chessboard of international espionage with his family in constant danger, Guy Trent becomes embroiled in moves and countermoves which may mean life or death for Western scientists.

TIGER TIGER
Frank Ryan

A young man involved in drugs is found murdered. This is the first event which will draw Detective Inspector Sandy Woodings into a whirlpool of murder and deceit.

CAROLINE MINUSCULE
Andrew Taylor

Caroline Minuscule, a medieval script, is the first clue to the whereabouts of a cache of diamonds. The search becomes a deadly kind of fairy story in which several murders have an other-worldly quality.

LONG CHAIN OF DEATH
Sarah Wolf

During the Second World War four American teenagers from the same town join the Army together. Forty-two years later, the son of one of the soldiers realises that someone is systematically wiping out the families of the four men.

THE LISTERDALE MYSTERY
Agatha Christie

Twelve short stories ranging from the light-hearted to the macabre, diverse mysteries ingeniously and plausibly contrived and convincingly unravelled.

TO BE LOVED
Lynne Collins

Andrew married the woman he had always loved despite the knowledge that Sarah married him for reasons of her own. So much heartache could have been avoided if only he had known how vital it was to be loved.

ACCUSED NURSE
Jane Converse

Paula found herself accused of a crime which could cost her her job, her nurse's reputation, and even the man she loved, unless the truth came to light.

BUTTERFLY MONTANE
Dorothy Cork

Parma had come to New Guinea to marry Alec Rivers, but she found him completely disinterested and that overbearing Pierce Adams getting entirely the wrong idea about her.

HONOURABLE FRIENDS
Janet Daley

Priscilla Burford is happily married when she meets Junior Environment Minister Alistair Thurston. Inevitably, sexual obsession and political necessity collide.

WANDERING MINSTRELS
Mary Delorme

Stella Wade's career as a concert pianist might have been ruined by the rudeness of a famous conductor, so it seemed to her agent and benefactor. Even Sir Nicholas fails to see the possibilities when John Tallis falls deeply in love with Stella.

MORNING IS BREAKING
Lesley Denny

The growing frenzy of war catapults Diane Clements into a clandestine marriage and separation with a German refugee.

LAST BUS TO WOODSTOCK
Colin Dexter

A girl's body is discovered huddled in the courtyard of a Woodstock pub, and Detective Chief Inspector Morse and Sergeant Lewis are hunting a rapist and a murderer.

THE STUBBORN TIDE
Anne Durham

Everyone advised Carol not to grieve so excessively over her cousin's death. She might have followed their advice if the man she loved thought that way about her, but another girl came first in his affections.